깃발

도서출판 아시아에서는 《바이링궐 에디션 한국 현대 소설》을 기획하여 한국의 우수한 문학을 주제별로 엄선해 국내외 독자들에게 소개합니다. 이 기획은 국내외 우수한 번역가들이 참여하여 원작의 품격을 최대한 살렸습니다. 문학을 통해 아시아의 정체성과 가치를 살피는 데 주력해 온 도서출판 아시아는 한국인의 삶을 넓고 깊게 이해하는 데 이 기획이 기여하기를 기대합니다.

Asia Publishers present some of the very best modern Korean literature to readers worldwide through its new Korean literature series 〈Bi-lingual Edition Modern Korean Literature〉. We are proud and happy to offer it in the most authoritative translation by renowned translators of Korean literature. We hope that this series helps to build solid bridges between citizens of the world and Koreans through rich in-depth understanding of Korea.

바이링궐 에디션 한국 현대 소설 019

Bi-lingual Edition Modern Korean Literature 019

The Flag

홍희담
깃발

Hong Hee-dam

ASIA
PUBLISHERS

Contents

깃발

The Flag

1

유리창이 덜커덩 하는 소리에 순분은 눈을 떴다. 열어
둔 창 틈으로 빗물이 흘러 들어와 벽을 적시고 있었다. 문
틈에 부딪친 빗물이 순분의 머리 위에 떨어졌다. 그 차가
움에 순분은 아직도 남아 있는 잠기운을 떨쳐냈다. 빗줄
기가 거세어졌다. 순분은 일어나 창문을 닫았다. 부엌에
서 달그락거리는 소리가 들렸다. 장지문 너머로 동생들의
코고는 소리도 들렸다. 어머니가 아침 준비를 하고 있었
다. 선라이트로 얼기설기 막아놓은 틈새로 빗물이 새어
들어와 구석을 적셨다. 두 사람이 들어서면 꽉 차는 조그

1

Sunbun woke to the rattling of panes. Raindrops were dripping in through an open window, wetting the wall beneath. Bouncing off the sill, they landed on her head. They were so cold that Sunbun was instantly wide-awake. Now it was raining even harder. Sunbun got up and closed the window. She could hear the clatter of pots and pans from the kitchen. Her younger siblings were snoring behind the sliding paper door. Her mother was cooking breakfast. Raindrops were falling through the cracks between patches of sunlight,[1] wetting the kitchen

마한 부엌이었다. 어머니가 말했다.

"하늘도 노하셨겠지. 웬수 놈들……"

순분은 쭈그리고 앉아 파를 다듬었다.

"한창 딸기 철인데……"

혼잣말처럼 어머니가 뇌까렸다.

이맘때면 인근 밭에서 딸기를 받아 팔아오던 어머니였다. 도시가 꽉꽉 막힌 지 벌써 3일째였다. 어머니는 혹 뚫린 곳이 있는지 아침마다 외곽 지대를 서성거려보았다. 어제는 딸기밭이 보이는 야산까지 올라갔다.

"……아이구. 죽을 뻔했다야. 총을 멘 군인들이 새까맣게 늘어서 있드라. 걸음아 나 살려라 하고 내뺐는데 뒤에서 총을 쏘아대지 않겠니. 저승길이 오락가락하드라."

밥솥에서 구수한 냄새가 났다. 순분이 말했다.

"또 보리를 많이 넣었나 보네."

"먹을 쌀도 얼마 안 남았어. 니 사장인가 하는 작자는 코빼기도 안 보이냐?"

"벌써 도망갔대나 봐."

"난리 나면 있는 놈들이 먼저 도망간다니까……"

순분이가 다니는 방직 회사는 그리 큰 편이 못 되었다. 큰 회사의 하청을 맡고 있었다. 50여 명의 근로자들이 한

floor here and there. Their kitchen was so tiny it could barely accommodate two people. Sunbun's mother said, "Even Heaven must be angry. What enemies..."

Sunbun squatted on the floor and began trimming scallions.

"It's strawberry season, but..." Mother muttered to herself.

She used to get strawberries from nearby farms and sell them in the city at this time of year. It had been three days since the city was completely blocked off. Every morning Mother explored the outskirts to see if any road was open. Yesterday, she climbed the hill, from which she could look down at the strawberry fields in the distance.

"Gees, I could have died. Soldiers in dark uniforms stood in a row, holding guns in their hands. I ran for dear life, but they started shooting at me. The road to the next world started flickering in front of my eyes."

A savory aroma came from the rice cooker. Sunbun said, "You've mixed in a lot of barley again, haven't you?"

"There's not much rice left. The guy who's supposed to be the owner of your company hasn't

달 꼬박 일해야 8만 원도 안 되었다. 그 돈이 순분네 식구에겐 고정 수입원이었다. 어머니와 순분이 그리고 동생 둘이 먹는 곡식 값이 반을 차지했고, 연탄과 전기세 수도세를 제하고 나면 남는 것이 없었다. 어머니가 노점상을 해서 버는 돈으로 간신히 동생들 공부를 시켰다. 순분네가 바라는 것은 조그만 구멍가게 하나 세를 얻어 어머니가 이리저리 쫓겨 다니지 않았으면 하는 바람이었다.

"쟤들 깨워라. 학교 안 간다고 늦잠이나 퍼질러 자고…… 난리도 이런 난리가 없구먼."

하면서 어머니가 혀를 끌끌 찼다. 동생들을 깨워 아침밥을 먹고 순분은 집을 나섰다.

비가 걷히어 아침이 반짝거렸다. 오월의 공기가 상쾌했다. 나무 잎사귀들은 물을 머금어 싱싱했고 꽃들은 빰 비비며 피어나고 있었다. 아직 이른 시간이라 시위 차량은 뜸했다. 앞서서 자전거를 타고 가던 남자가 힐끗 돌아다 보았다. 속력을 늦추었다. 순분이가 다가가자 남자가 말했다.

"도청 가시죠?"

순분은 대답을 않고 계속 걸어갔다. 남자가 천천히 페달을 밟으며 다시 말했다.

showed up yet?"

"I heard he already ran away."

"When something happens, the haves run away first..."

Sunbun had been working at a medium-sized textile company that subcontracted for a bigger company. A month's salary for each of the fifty workers was less than 80,000 *won*, even when they worked as hard as they could. That was the only source of regular income for Sunbun's family. Half of it paid for food for the family—Mother, Sunbun, and her two younger siblings—and the other half went to briquettes, electricity, and water. What Mother made from her street stall barely paid for the younger children's tuition. Sunbun's family wished they could rent a small store so that Mother didn't have to move her stall around to avoid crackdowns.

"Wake them up! Oversleeping 'cause they don't have to go to school... What a lot of trouble war is!"

Mother clucked her tongue: Tchick tchick! After waking up her younger siblings and eating breakfast, Sunbun left the house.

The rain had stopped and the morning was brilliant. The May air was refreshing. The wet leaves were glistening, and flowers were beginning to

"꽤 먼 거리잖아요. 뒤에 타세요. 안전하게 모셔다드릴
게요."

순분은 주저하다가 자전거 뒤에 올라탔다. 손을 어찌할
까, 하다가 속력을 내는 바람에 저도 모르게 남자 허리께
를 붙잡았다. 시민들은 걸어서 혹은 자전거를 타고 도청
으로 갔다. 도로는 깨끗했다. 남자가 말했다.

"말끔하죠?"

"네."

"어제 궐기대회가 끝나고, 남아서 청소를 했어요. 누가
하란 것도 아닌데 많이들 거들더군요."

도시 중심부로 가까이 갈수록 전쟁을 겪고 난 흔적이
역력했다. 깨진 유리창이며 시커멓게 그은 벽, 그리고 불
타 버린 공공건물들……

"저 봐요." 하면서 남자가 턱으로 밑을 가리켰다. 비에
젖어 선연히 드러난 핏자국이었다. 핏자국을 피하느라고
자전거가 삐끗했다. 남자가 말했다.

"저렇게 시뻘겋게 살아 있는데…… 무기 반납하자는 놈
들은 저런 것도 안 보이나 보지요? 대개 학생놈들인데 정
말 총으로 갈겨버리고 싶데요."

남자가 페달을 마구 밟았다.

bloom, rubbing their cheeks together. Because it was still early, there weren't many cars with demonstrators. A man on a bicycle in front of her cast a quick backward glance. He slowed down. As Sunbun approached, he said,

"You're going to the governor's office complex, aren't you?"

Not answering, Sunbun kept walking. Pedaling slowly, the man said again, "It's pretty far, isn't it? Get on back! I'll take you there safe and sound."

After a moment's hesitation, Sunbun got on the back of the bicycle. She was wondering what to do with her hands when the bike began speeding, forcing her to hold onto the man's waist. People were walking or biking to the governor's office. The streets were clean. The man commented, "It's really clean, isn't it?"

"Yes."

"We stayed behind to clean the streets after the rally yesterday. Although nobody was asking us to do it, people rushed to volunteer."

The closer they got to downtown, the more obvious it was that there had been a war. Broken glass, charred walls, and burned-out public buildings...

"Look at that!"

"좀 천천히 달려요. 무서워요."

순분이가 소리치자 남자가 뒤를 돌아보며 씩 웃었다.

"무섭긴 뭐가 무서워요. 씽씽 달리는 자가용도 없겠다, 택시도 없겠다, 정말 자전거가 교통수단이 되니까 우리 같은 사람들 살맛이 나네요. 아가씨 같은 분도 태워줄 수 있고요."

평소엔 낯선 사람과 말도 못 하는 주제에 어떻게 자전 거까지 얻어 탈 수 있나, 하고 순분은 자신의 대담성에 놀 라워했다. 그러나 낯선 사람들이 아니었다. 도시 전체가 일치감을 느끼고 있었다. 모두가 하나였다. 모두가 보고 웃었다. 피어나는 기쁨에 손에 손을 잡았다.

남자는 무기를 어떻게 습득하게 되었으며, 그 전쟁에서 (라고 남자는 표현했다) 자신은 어떤 역할을 했으며, 그 무 기로 공수특전단을 어떻게 통쾌하게 물리쳤는가를 신이 나서 이야기했다.

"……아가씨는 잘 모르겠지만 공수특전단이라는 게 단 순한 군인이 아니지요. 명령만 내리면 어디에나 어느 사 람이나 쑥밭을 만들든가 살해하든가 무엇이든지 해치우 는 살인마들이지요. 말하자면 특수부대죠. 전쟁이 났을 때 적의 심장부에 투입되어 효과적인 전투를 수행하는 임

The man pointed with his chin to ground. It was a bloodstain, vividly red after the rain. The bicycle swerved a bit as the man tried not to drive over it. He said, "How amazingly red and alive... I guess those who propose turning in our gunds haven't seen it? They're mostly students. I almost felt like shooting them myself."

The man pedaled wildly.

"Please go slower. I'm scared," Sunbun cried. He turned around and smiled.

"What are you scared of? There are no private cars or taxis. Now that bicycles are the major means of transportation, life is great for guys like me. We can give a ride to a lady like you."

Sunbun was actually surprised at her own audacity in getting on a stranger's bicycle. Ordinarily, she wouldn't even speak with strangers. But he wasn't a stranger. The entire city was feeling united. All were one. People looked at each other and smiled. They joyfully held hands.

The man talked excitedly about how they had acquired weapons, what role he played in the war—that was his word—, and how proud they were when they vanquished the airborne troops.

"...You might not know this, but the airborne

무를 맡고 있지요. 그들은 아군의 승패와 관련 없이 적진 속에서 죽음을 불사하는 철의 인간들이지요. 이런 임무를 같은 동족에게 해치웠으니 말이나 됩니까? 아마 공수부대가 생겨난 이후로 세계적으로도 이런 일은 없을 겁니다."

순분은 몸을 떨었다. 그녀도 보아서 안다.

그날은 18일, 피의 일요일이었다. 순분이가 다니던 야학은 일요일엔 예배를 보았다. 예배를 마치고 친구들과 어울려 중국집에서 점심을 먹었다. 노닥거리다가 버스를 탔다. 네 시쯤이나 되었을까, 버스가 공용터미널 부근에서 멈추어 섰다. 시위 군중들이 모여들어 빠져나갈 수가 없었다. 버스에 탔던 사람들이 내리는 바람에 순분이도 따라 내렸다. 전경들이 쏘아대는 최루탄에 이미 부근은 매캐한 연기로 가득 찼다. 금남로와 소방서 쪽에서 군중들이 계속 몰려오고 있었다. 순분은 군중들과 섞여 꼼짝할 수가 없었다. 갑자기 여기저기서 비명 소리가 터져 나왔다. 쓰라린 눈을 가까스로 떴다. 어디서 나타났는지 얼룩무늬 군복을 입은 군인들이 날뛰고 있었다(나중에 그들이 공수특전단이라는 것을 알았다). 공수특전단들은 무조건 곤봉을 휘둘렀다. 머리고 가슴이고 닥치는 대로 내질렀

ranger-commando force isn't just a simple army. They're cutthroats who, if ordered, would completely turn any place into ruins, kill anybody, and destroy everything. In other words, they're special troops. They're thrown into the heart of enemy territory when war breaks out, and they're expected to win. That's their task. They're iron men, ready to die in the middle of the enemy's camp regardless of the battle's outcome. How absurd that they carried out their duties against their own countrymen! There's probably no precedent for this kind of incident in the entire history of the airborne troops."

Sunbun shuddered. She knew, because she had seen it all.

The 18th was a bloody Sunday. That day there was a service at the night school Sunbun attended. Afterward she had lunch with her friends at a Chinese restaurant. She got on the bus after hanging out with them. The bus stopped near the public terminal, but couldn't go any further because the street was full of demonstrators. Sunbun got off, following the passengers. The area was full of pungent smoke because of the tear gas canisters the combat policemen had been firing. Crowds kept pouring out of

19

다. 그들과 맞닿아 있던 군중들이 순식간에 피를 토하고 쓰러졌다. 손을 뻗치는 사람에게 가차없이 대검으로 배를 쑤셨다. 누군가가 순분의 팔을 끌어당겼다. 그녀는 골목길로 내달리다가 앞사람을 좇아 건물 속으로 숨어들었다. 서너 명이 숨을 죽이고 숨어 있었다. 창밖으로 군용 트럭이 달려오는 것이 보였다. 트럭이 멈추어 서자 이미 포승으로 묶은 사람들을 차에다 던져 올렸다. 올라온 즉시 옷을 찢어대더니 등 뒤를 개머리판으로 계속 난타했다. 어떤 공수특전단원들은 대검으로 청년의 등을 쑤시고는 다리를 잡아 질질 끌어서 트럭 위에 던졌다. 노인 하나가 끌려가는 청년을 뒤따르며 손을 저었다. 공수특전단은 한 손에 청년의 발을 잡은 채로 대검으로 노인을 내리쳤다. 노인은 피를 뒤집어쓰며 고꾸라졌다. 거리에는 일시에 살기가 맴돌았다. 시뻘건 칼날이 햇빛에 번들거렸다. 트럭 안은 던져진 시체들로 가득 들어찼다. 트럭이 움직였다. 그리고 어디론가 사라졌다.

비명과 흐느낌이 요란했다. 순분은 온몸이 얼어붙어 있었다. 숨어 있던 사람들이 움직이는 대로 그녀도 따라 건물에서 나왔다. 사람들이 길바닥에 주저앉아 통곡하고 있었다.

Geumnam-ro Street and the fire station. Sunbun couldn't move, stuck in the middle of the crowd. Suddenly she heard shrieks here and there. She could barely open her eyes because they were stinging so much. Soldiers in combat fatigues appeared out of the blue on a wild rampage. She later found out they were airborne troops. They were swinging their clubs at random targets. It didn't matter whether the clubs fell on heads or breasts. People nearby immediately threw up blood and fell down. Those who stretched out their arms had their bellies pierced by bayonets. Someone pulled Sunbun by the elbow. She dashed into a nearby alley and then blindly followed the person in front of her into a building. Several people were already hiding there, holding their breath. They could see a military truck rushing by outside the window. The truck stopped, and people already tied up with rope were thrown onto it. As soon as they were on the truck, their shirts were torn off and their backs beaten indiscriminately with gunstocks. One of the airborne troops poked a young man in the back with a bayonet, dragged him by his legs, and threw him onto the truck. An old man followed the young man, waving his hands. The sol-

"악귀들이야, 악귀들."

"인간의 탈을 쓰고 어찌 저럴 수가 있단 말인가."

"같은 민족끼리 어찌 저럴 수가."

"이대로 죽을 수는 없어."

온 거리는 피의 강, 통곡의 바다였다.

순분은 어떻게 집에 왔는지 모른다. 머리는 산발이었다. 신은 벗겨져 있었고 발바닥에서 피가 흘렀다. 온몸에 신열이 났다. 헛소리를 하며 이불을 뒤집어쓰고 벌벌 떨었다. 헛것이 보였다. 커다란 곤봉이 내리쳐지는 바람에 소스라쳐 놀라곤 했다. 날이 선 대검이 춤을 추며 그녀의 배를 쑤셨다. 주위는 온통 피바다였다. 옷깃에는 핏덩이가 엉겨 있어 손톱으로 긁어냈다. 살과 뼈가 분해되어 공중으로 훨훨 날아다녔다. 짓밟혀 생생한 시체 더미가 되어 땅 위에 굴러다녔다. 그녀는 손을 싹싹 빌었다. 젖가슴을 헤치고 죄가 없다고 가슴을 쥐어뜯었다.

"쥑일 놈들 쥑일 놈들……"

이따금 정신이 들 때면 어머니의 뇌까리는 소리가 들려왔다. 이틀을 그렇게 비몽사몽 헤맸다. 정신이 들면서 그녀가 느낀 것은 살아있는 것이 몹시 무섭다는 거였다. 숨쉬는 것마저 힘겨웠다. 육체는 넋이 빠져 로봇 같았다. 파

dier struck the old man with his bayonet, still holding the feet of the young man with his other hand. The old man fell on his face, blood spattering all over his body. The street was instantaneously filled with deadly fear. The bloody red blade was shining in the sunlight. The truck was full of bodies. It started to move. Then it disappeared.

There was loud crying and sobbing. Sunbun was completely frozen. As the people who were hiding with her began moving, she mechanically followed them out of the building. People were squatting and wailing on the street.

"Devils, devils."

"How could a human being do that?"

"How could our own people..."

"We cannot die like this."

The street was a sea of blood and howling.

Sunbun could not remember how she got home. Her hair was disheveled. Her shoes were gone and her soles were bleeding. She was feverish. Talking in delirium, she hid under a blanket, trembling wildly. She was in a trance. Feeling as if a club were striking her body, she was startled out of her wits. A bayonet with a sharp edge was dancing around her and poking her belly. A sea of blood surrounded

충류들이 사는 세계에 내팽개쳐진 것 같았다. 차라리 그
때 죽었으면, 하고 바라기도 했다. 죽음보다 더 무서운 생
생한 비명 소리와 칼부림과 찢긴 시체 더미. 그런 기억을
갖고 어떻게 온전히 살아갈 수 있을 것인가. 생명 한 줌
움켜쥐고 그녀는 이를 악문 채 일어섰다.

"듣고 있어요?"
하는 소리에 순분은 퍼뜩 정신을 차렸다. 남자가 얼굴을
돌리는 바람에 자전거가 삐끗했다. 다시 중심을 잡으며
말을 이었다.

"내 말을 들어보란 말예요. 중국집 배달원이 공수대원
과 싸워 이겼다면 누가 믿겠어요?"

"중국집 배달원요?"

"내가 바로 중국집 배달원이란 말입니다. 하하하."

남자의 목소리가 의기양양해져서 웃음소리도 마냥 허
풍스러웠다.

불타 버린 노동청을 지날 때 남자는 퉤, 하고 침을 뱉었다.

"노동청이 뭐 하는 덴지 정말 몰랐다구요. 높은 나리들
이나 들락거리는 덴 줄 알았지 뭡니까. 알구 보니 노동자
들을 위한 건물이라던데 이 근처에 오면 괜히 주눅이 들

her. She scratched the clotted blood from her clothes. Pieces of her flesh and bones flew around in the air. They were trampled on, became a heap of dead bodies, and then started rolling around all over the street. She was begging with folded hands, rubbing them together like crazy. Exposing her breasts and poking at them with her hands, she insisted she was innocent.

"Scoundrels, scoundrels..."

Whenever she emerged briefly from her torment, she could hear her mother muttering. In this state she drifted in and out of lucidity for two days. When she finally awoke, her first thought was that it was terrifying to be alive. It was hard even to breathe. Her body felt like a robot without a soul. She felt as if she had been thrown into a world of reptiles. She even wished that she had died during the commotion of that day. The vivid screams, swung swords, and heaps of torn bodies were scarier even than death. How could she live with such memories? Grasping at life, she gritted her teeth and tried to get up.

"Are you listening?"

Surprised, Sunbun returned to reality. The bicycle

곤 했지요. MBC도 불타고 세무서도 불났지만 여기 불탈 때가 제일 신나더군요. 그때 들어가 보았지요. 닥치는 대로 부수어버렸죠. 만세를 부르고 애국가도 합창을 했어요. 애국가를 부를 때 가슴이 뭉클하데요."

도청의 분수대가 보였다. 남자는 페달을 천천히 밟았다. 남자가 말을 이었다.

"머리털 나고 처음으로 애국가다운 애국가를 부른 듯한 느낌이 들었지요. 왜 다섯 시만 되면 애국가가 울려 퍼지잖아요. 길거리 가다가도 공연히 서서 들어야 하고, 극장에 가도 들어야 하잖아요. 애국은 이런 것이 아닌데, 하는 생각과 이럴 때의 애국은 마치 권력자들에게 아부하는 것 같아 기분도 안 좋지요. 그런데 그땐 그렇지가 않았어요. 정말 내가 애국자가 된 것 같아 눈물을 찔끔 흘렸지요."

자전거가 멈추었다. 순분은 자전거에서 내려왔다. 남자도 내려와 보조를 같이했다.

도청 앞 광장에 많은 사람들이 몰려들고 있었다. 그들 중에는 각동 단위로 몇백 명씩 집결하여 구호를 쓴 피켓과 플래카드를 쳐들고 구호를 외치고 노래를 부르기도 했다. 도청 주변 담벽에는 각종 플래카드가 울긋불긋 붙어 있었다.

swerved momentarily as the man turned towards her. Balancing again, he continued: "Listen to me. Who would believe me when I say a delivery boy from a Chinese restaurant prevailed against airborne troops?"

"A delivery boy from a Chinese restaurant?"

"I am that delivery boy from a Chinese restaurant, hahaha."

He said this in high spirits, his laughter tinged with bragging.

When they were passing by the charred building of the regional office of the Ministry of Labor, he spat on the road.

"I really didn't know what kind of place this was. I thought it was a place where only high officials come and go. I hear it's a building for workers, but I used to get discouraged for no reason whenever I was near it. Although both the MBC building and the Revenue Office building were burned as well, it felt like the most wonderful thing when this building was burned down. I went into it just before. I broke things inside it. I cheered and sang the national anthem. When I sang the national anthem, I felt deeply moved."

They could see the fountain in front of the gover-

민주시민 만세

살인마…… 찢어 죽여라

노동삼권 보장하라

어용노조 물러가라

비상계엄 해제하라

유신잔당 물러가라

휴교령 철폐

농협관료 물러가라

죽을 때까지 싸운다

해방의 그날까지

광주 꼬뮨 만세

빨간색과 검은색, 파란색 페인트로 그려진 현수막은 마치 함성과도 같았다. 도청 앞 광장 맞은편 상무관을 가리키며 남자가 말했다.

"저기 가서 분향을 합시다."

상무관에는 많은 시체가 무명천에 덮여 진열되어 있었다. 관이 부족하여 아직 입관되지 못한 시체도 수십 구 있었으며 무명천 위로 검붉은 핏자국들이 배어 나와 있었다. 분향대가 입구에 설치되어 있었다. 남자가 향을 피워

nor's office complex. The man slowed his pedaling. He continued:

"I felt as if I was singing the national anthem for the first time since I was born. You know, the national anthem fills the street at five p.m. everyday. You have to stop and listen to it for no reason, and you're forced to listen even in theatres. You feel this can't be truly patriotic, that this kind of patriotism is unpleasant because it feels like kissing the asses of the powerful. But at that moment, it was different. I started tearing up, feeling like a true patriot."

The bicycle stopped. Sunbun got off. The man got off, too, and walked beside her.

Crowds were pouring into the plaza in front of the governor's office. Groups of several hundred people from the same city district had gathered here and there, holding placards and picket signs with slogans on them, and they were shouting slogans and singing songs together. Various colorful placards were hanging from the wall nearby.

Hurrah, Democratic Citizens!
Rip XXX, the Homicidal Maniac, to Shreds!
Guarantee Three Basic Labor Rights!
Down with Company Unions!

꽂았다. 순분이도 따라 했다. 고개를 숙일 때 오열이 터져 나왔다. 정신이 아찔했다. 남자가 어깨를 받쳐주었다. 관을 부여안고 통곡하는 소리가 상무관을 메우고 있었다. 가슴이 막혀 미처 목젖을 빠져나오지 못한 오열 소리는 구천을 헤매는 영령들의 소리 같기도 했다. 슬픔도 극도에 달하면 울음소리가 제대로 나오지 않는 것일까. 확인하려고 내놓은 얼굴은 차마 볼 수가 없었다. 대검으로 난자되어 귀에서 턱으로 잘린 얼굴도 있었고 목젖이 너덜거리는 얼굴, 이마를 정면으로 찔린 얼굴은 눈을 부릅뜨고 이를 악물고 있었다. 밖으로 나오면서 남자가 말했다.

"그래도 저 시체들은 다행한 편이에요. 어디로 끌려갔는지, 어디서 죽었는지 확인되지 않은 시체들은 또 얼마나 많겠어요?"

그의 눈가에 파르르 경련이 일었다. 그의 얼굴에 어떤 결의 같은 것이 나타났다. 그가 말했다.

"저렇게 죽어갔는데 어떻게 무기를 반납하라는 겁니까? 지금 이 시점에서 무기를 반납하라는 것은 우리 시민의 피를 팔아먹는 행위예요. 절대 반납해서는 안 돼요." 하면서 남자가 다급하게 걸음을 떼어 놓았다. 순분이가 말했다.

Lift Martial law!

Down with Remnants of the Yushin!

Reopen Schools!

Down with Agricultural Cooperative Officials!

We'll Fight to the Death.

Until the Day of Liberation

Hurrah, Gwangju Commune!

The placards with letters in red, black, and blue paint were like outcries. Pointing to the Sangmu building across the street, the man said, "Let's go there and offer incense."

Inside there were many rows of bodies covered with cotton cloth. Because there weren't enough caskets, dozens of bodies hadn't been put in coffins yet. Some cloth was smeared with blood. There was an incense burner stand at the entrance. The man burned some incense. Sunbun did the same. While she was bowing her head, she burst into tears. She felt dizzy. The man supported her by holding her shoulder. The Sangmu building was filled with people's lamentations over the dead. Their cries, which could barely escape their throats because they were so constricted by smoldering heartache, sounded like the voices of spirits wandering in the under-

"자전거는 어떻게 하고요?"

"지금 자전거가 문제예요? 도청으로 들어가야만 되겠어요. 아가씨, 그럼 여기서 헤어져요. 또 만날 수 있겠죠."

걸음이 빨라지다가 이윽고는 달려가는 남자의 뒷모습을 한동안 바라보았다. 도청 정문 쪽에 많은 사람이 모여 있었다. 그의 모습이 인파에 가려 구별할 수가 없었다. 순분은 걸음을 떼어 놓았다. 주변의 담벽에는 여러 가지 선전 구호가 적힌 플래카드, 대자보 등이 나붙었으며 잔혹하게 죽은 시체와 부상자들 그리고 병원에서 지금 죽어가고 있는 사람들의 모습을 담은, 급히 현상한 듯한 흑백 사진이 무수히 걸려 있었다. 수습위원회의 투항주의적 자세를 맹렬히 비난하는 문구도 보였다. 순분은 수습이라는 문구 자체가 눈에 거슬렸다. 순분이 앞에서 사진을 보고 있던 단발머리 여자애가 울고 있는지 어깨가 들먹거렸다. 얼굴을 앞으로 가져갔다. 영순이었다. 그녀들은 거의 똑같이 이름을 부르며 얼싸안았다.

"살아 있었구나."

눈물을 훔쳐 내며 영순이가 말했다. 같은 공장의 근로자였고 야학에도 같이 다녔다. 그녀들은 최루탄 때문에 잎이 시들시들한 플라타너스 밑에 앉았다.

world. 'Perhaps one can't even cry when one is extremely sad?' Sunbun did not have the heart to do more than glance at the faces that remained uncovered so people could identify them. There was a face cut from ear to chin with a bayonet, a face with a shredded Adam's apple, and a face with glaring eyes and clenched teeth that was slashed across the forehead. On their way out the man said, "Those were the lucky ones. How many others were dragged off and killed who knows where!"

The skin around his eyes was quivering, but he was resolute. He said, "People died like that. How could we just turn over our weapons? Handing them over at this point would mean betraying the blood of our citizens. We must not return them."

The man hurried on his way. Sunbun asked, "What are you going to do with your bicycle?"

"Who cares about the bicycle? I have to get to the governor's office. Let's say good-bye here. I hope we meet again."

Sunbun stared at the man's back as he walked away faster and faster and eventually started running. Many people had gathered around the main entrance to the governor's office. She could no longer make him out, as he disappeared into the

영순네 집은 산수동 밑에 있었다. 그날 18일, 순분이들과 헤어진 영순은 공수대원들을 피해 가까스로 집에 도착했다. 식구들은 방에 있지 않고 연탄과 허드레 물건을 넣어둔 광 속에 숨어 있었다. 주인 식구들과 같이 있었다. 영순이가 막 숨고 난 직후 담 위로 청년 둘이 뛰어올랐다. 한 청년이 미처 다리를 들어올리지 못했을 때 군홧발 소리가 울렸다. 허리 반쯤만 보이던 청년이 으윽 소리를 내더니 담 밖으로 떨어졌다. 한 청년은 마당으로 뛰어내렸다. 미처 피할 틈도 없이 공수대원이 문을 박차고 뛰어들어 왔다. 붉은 얼굴에 눈은 살기를 번뜩이며 청년의 뒤꼭지를 향해 곤봉을 내리쳤다. 청년은 피를 토하며 나동그라졌다. 공수대원은 머리채를 휘어잡고 질질 끌고 나갔다. 문 앞에서 공수대원이 소리쳤다.

"데모하는 년놈들은 모두 죽여버린다."

영순이의 이야기를 들으면서 순분은 그날의 공포가 다시금 되살아났다. 눈물을 손등으로 씻으며 영순이가 말했다.

"숨어서 다 보았어. 우린 그날 밤 방에서 못 잤어. 공포로 밤을 꼬박 새웠지."

분수대 앞에는 많은 사람들이 몰려 혼잡을 이루고 있었다. 궐기대회는 아직 열리지 않았다. 영순이가 마지막 눈

crowd. Sunbun began walking. Placards with slogans, wall posters, and many black-and-white photographs of those cruelly murdered, injured, or dying in the hospital beds were posted on nearby walls. There were also words harshly critical of the capitulating attitude of the committee entrusted with control of the situation. Sunbun didn't like the phrase "control of the situation." The shoulders of a girl with bobbed hair, who was looking at the photographs in front of Sunbun, were shaking. She must have been crying. Sunbun went closer. It was Yeong-sun. They called each other's names almost simultaneously and hugged each other.

"You are alive!" Yeong-sun said, wiping away tears. They worked at the same factory and attended the same night school. They sat down under an American sycamore tree whose leaves had wilted from the tear gas.

Yeong-sun's house was located at the foot of Sansu-dong. On the 18th, Yeong-sun had barely managed to get home after parting from Sunbun and other friends. When she arrived, her family wasn't in their rooms, but hiding in the storehouse in which they kept briquettes and odds and ends. Their landlord's family was there, too. No sooner

물을 씻어 내며 말했다.

"우리도 이러고만 있을 수 없잖아."

"어떻게 해야 할지 모르겠어."

"야학에 가보자. 혹시 친구들이 있을지도 모르잖아."

"그게 좋겠구나. 같이 모이면 좋은 생각이 떠오를지도 모르니까."

그녀들은 손을 꼬옥 잡고 야학 건물이 있는 광천동 쪽으로 걸어갔다. 야학은 낡은 목조건물 이 층에 있었다. 층계를 오르내릴 적마다 삐그덕거렸다. 모서리가 닳아져 잘못 디디면 미끄러지기 일쑤였다. 그런 계단을 둘이는 단숨에 올라갔다. 문이 빠끔히 열려 있었다.

"드디어 나타난다." 하면서 얼굴들이 나타났다. 전남제사에 다니는 형자와 미숙이, 그리고 순분이와 같은 방직 회사의 철순이었다.

"순분아, 방금 니 이야기를 하고 있었어."

미숙이가 말했다.

"얼마나 걱정했는지 몰라. 그날 공용터미널에서 너를 보았었거든. 공수대원들이 그 난리를 치고 난 후 너를 찾으니까 안 보이잖아. 혹시나 하고 얼마나 애태웠다구."

미숙이는 순분이의 손을 잡은 채 계속 말하였다.

had Yeong-sun hid in the storehouse than two young men jumped onto the wall of their house. While one of them was still pulling himself up, they could hear the tramp of military boots. The young man, half his upper body visible, let out a cry and fell behind the wall. The other young man jumped down into the yard. One of the airborne troops kicked the gate open and dashed in. His face flushed and his eyes bright with murderous intent, he brought his club down on the crown of the young man's head. The young man tumbled down, vomiting blood. The soldier held him by the hair and dragged him out. At the gate he yelled, "I'll kill all you demonstrating punks and bitches."

Listening to Yeong-sun's story, Sunbun remembered her fear that day. Wiping away tears with the back of her hand, Yeong-sun said, "We could see everything from where we were hiding. We couldn't sleep in our rooms that night. We stayed up all night terrified."

The plaza in front of the fountain was bustling with crowds. The rally hadn't started yet. Wiping away tears for the last time, Yeong-sun said, "We can't just sit still, can we?"

"I don't know what to do."

미숙이는 전날(17일) 늦게 고향인 해남으로 내려갔다. 2년 동안 30만 원짜리 적금을 부어온 것이 만기가 되어 처음으로 큰돈을 갖고 고향으로 내려간 것이다. 고향 집에는 늙으신 부모와 오빠, 중학교에 다니는 동생이 살고 있었다. 포도밭 500평과 논 세 마지기를 소작하여 근근이 살아가고 있었다. 아버지는 중풍으로 누워 있어 일을 할 수가 없었다. 아버지는 30만 원을 받아 들고 눈물만 흘렸다. 어머니는 부엌에서 치마폭을 적셨고 오빠는 미숙이의 거친 손을 꼭 잡고 눈물을 삼켰다. 이튿날 오빠와 같이 올라왔다. 가톨릭농민회 회원인 오빠는 19일 광주 호남동 성당에서 열리는 농민대회에 참석하기 위해서였다. 그들이 공용터미널에 내렸을 때가 네 시쯤이었다. 그 엄청난 학살 장면을 목격한 그들은 공포에 떨며 미숙이 자취방에 와서 하룻밤을 꼬박 새웠다. 이튿날 농민대회에 참석하고 돌아온 오빠는 화가 치밀어 있었다.

전남 각지에서 몰려온 농민들이 전날의 학살 소식을 듣고 흥분했다는 것이다. 이대로 시내로 진출해 공수대원들과 붙어보자고 아우성이었다. 농민들은 낫과 곡괭이 등을 갖고 오지 못한 것을 안타까워하며 무기 될 만한 것을 찾아보기도 했다. 그러나 농민 운동권 지도부에서 반대를

"Let's go to the night school building. We might find our friends there."

"That's a good idea. We can think of something together."

Holding hands tightly, they walked towards the night school at Gwangcheon-dong. The school was on the second floor of an old wooden building. The stairs creaked under their feet and the edges of the steps were so worn that people often slipped if they weren't careful. They rushed up the stairs in one breath. The door was ajar.

"Here they are, finally!"

With this shout, faces became visible. There was Hyeong-ja and Misuk from the Jeonnam Spinning Company as well as Cheol-sun who worked at the same textile company as Sunbun.

"Sunbun, we were just talking about you," Misuk said.

"We were so worried about you. I saw you at the public terminal. After that horrible attack by the airborne troops, I looked for you in vain. I was so worried," Misuk continued, grasping Sunbun's hand.

Misuk had been to Haenam, her hometown the previous day, i.e. May seventeenth. As her two-year, three-hundred-thousand-*won* savings-by-installment

하고 나섰다. 엄청난 물리력을 갖고 있는 공수대원들과 붙는다는 것은 현시점에서 무모한 행동이다, 지금 농민회 역량으로선 그들을 물리칠 힘도 없을뿐더러 조직이 파괴될 위험도 있다, 더군다나 확대계엄으로 체포의 위험도 있다, 어차피 지는 싸움일 텐데 사태를 관망하며 각자 소신껏 행동한다, 등등의 결정이 내려졌다. 농민회원들은 격렬하게 반대했지만 지도부의 결정을 바꿀 수는 없었다. 지도부는 잠적해버렸다. 농민회원들은 어찌할 바를 모르고 뿔뿔이 흩어져 버렸다.

오빠는 거친 숨을 내쉬며 지도부 욕을 해댔다. 미숙이도 덩달아 화가 치밀어 올랐다. 그녀가 물었다.

"오빠, 지는 싸움이라니, 그것이 뭔 말이야?"

"글쎄 말이다. 싸워보지도 않고 진다고 결정을 내리는 것이 지도부의 할 일이냐? 그런 자들을 지도부라고 떠받들어 왔으니, 아이구 속 터진다, 속 터져."

"지도부를 빼버리고 농민회원들끼리 단합하면 될 거 아니야?"

"그게 그렇지가 않더라구. 조직인가 뭔가 하는 것에 속해 있으면 거기에 따르게 마련이지. 그러니까 지도부가 중요하다는 거야."

account had matured, she went home for the first time with a large sum of money. Her elderly parents, older brother, and younger sibling, a middle school student, were at home. They were barely scraping by, doing tenant farming of a five-hundred-*pyeong* grape orchard and three-*majigi* rice paddy.[2] Her father, bedridden from a stroke, couldn't work. When she gave him the money she had brought, he couldn't stop crying. Her mother's tears were dripping onto her skirt in the kitchen, and her brother was gulping back his own tears, holding tightly onto Misuk's rough hand. The next day, Misuk returned to Gwangju with her brother. A member of the Catholic Farmers Association, he was going to attend a farmers' rally. When they arrived at the public terminal in Gwangju, it was around 4 P.M. After witnessing that atrocious massacre, they stayed up all night at Misuk's boarding house. Her brother came back to her room extremely angry the next day after attending the rally.

He said that the farmers who had come from all over Jeollanam-do were extremely upset at news of the massacre. They were clamoring to go downtown immediately and fight the airborne troops. Regretting that they didn't bring their sickles and

오빠는 방구석에 처박혀 있을 수가 없었던지 집을 나가 버렸다. 갖고 올라온 가방을 그대로 놔둔 것으로 보아 고향 집에도 내려가지 않았을 터인데, 그 후로 종무소식이었다.

미숙이가 한숨을 포옥 내쉬며 말했다.

"해방이 되었는데도 안 나타나니까 자꾸만 이상한 생각이 들잖아. 혹시나 해서 병원이란 병원은 다 찾아보았고 상무관에도 가보았지만 찾을 수가 없었어. 고향 집에 내려갔나 하고 알아보고 싶어도 연락할 수가 있어야지. 고향 집에도 안 갔다면 오빠는……"

미숙이는 말을 잇지 못하고 고개를 떨어뜨렸다. 형자가 미숙이의 어깨를 쓸어주었다.

"지는 싸움이라고 말했던 자들, 지금쯤 무슨 낯을 하고 있을까?"

형자가 말했다.

"윤 선생님도 그런 말을 했어."

"윤 선생님이? 어떻게 그럴 수가?"

모두들 눈을 동그랗게 떴다.

강학들 중에 윤강일은 특별한 데가 있었다. 전남대학교 사학과 3학년 때 데모 주동자가 되어 감방 생활을 했었다.

pickaxes, they began looking for anything they could use as weapons. But the leadership was opposed: "It is reckless at this point to fight with the airborne troops with their enormous firepower; Currently, the Farmers Association not only lacks the capacity to beat them but we would also be risking the destruction of our organization if we fight; besides, because martial law has been extended, we could be all arrested; it's a losing battle, so we should just follow the situation. Each individual should act according to his conscience." Although the members were fiercely opposed to this decision, they could not persuade the leadership to change. After making the announcement, the leaders simply disappeared. Members dispersed, not knowing what to do.

Misuk's brother was fuming and cursing the leaders. Misuk felt angry, too. She asked, "Brother, what do they mean by 'a losing battle'?"

"Who knows? To decide we'll lose without even trying—is that what leaders are supposed to do? I can't believe I've been looking up to those people. I'm so upset!"

"Couldn't the ordinary members have united without their leaders?"

공부가 끝나고 이따금 조촐한 간담회가 열리면 윤강일은 곧잘 감방 생활의 이모저모를 이야기하곤 했다. 눈에 핏발까지 세우며 이야기하는 그를 보고 있을라치면 나도 한번 감방 생활을 했으면, 하는 바람이 일 정도였다.

"감옥이 바깥과 차단되어 고독할 것 같지?" 하고 윤강일은 이미 대답을 준비한 물음을 물었다.

"그렇지가 않아. 절대로 고독하지가 않아."

하나의 커다란 집단으로서, 아무리 엄격하게 격리한다 하더라도 그들은 강한 연대감으로 맺어져 있다는 것이다. 연대는 두터운 벽도 파고든다. 벽은 살아 있어 말을 하기도 하고 혹은 쿵쿵 하는 신호로 의사를 소통하기도 한다. 한 마디의 말이나 한 번의 눈짓으로도 모두를 이해한다. 감옥은 갇혀 있는 것이 아니다. 사회를 진단하는 하나의 집단이다. 그것도 전투적인 집단이다, 하고 윤강일은 말했다. 또 하나의 노동자 집단도 전투적 집단이라고 덧붙여 말했다. 윤강일은 두 집단의 유사성을 여러 예를 들어 설명했다.

본래 인간에겐 양면성이 있다. 강함과 약함. 용기와 공포. 아름다움과 추함. 존엄성과 비열성. 이 두 집단에는 이런 양면성이 허용되지 않는다. 어느 한쪽만이 요구된

"It doesn't work that way. If you belong to an organization, you follow its leaders. That's why leadership is important."

Probably unable to sit still, Misuk's brother had gone out. Since he left behind the bag he had brought from home, he couldn't have gone back there, but Misuk hadn't been able to find him ever since.

Sighing deeply, Misuk said,

"Because he didn't show up even after the liberation, I couldn't help but worry. I've been to all the hospitals and even the Sangmu building just in case, but I couldn't find him. I wish I could check whether he's gone home or not, but it's impossible to do that now. If he didn't go home..."

Unable to continue, Misuk hung her head. Hyeong-ja patted her on the shoulder.

"Those who said this was a losing battle—I'd like to see their faces now," said Hyeong-ja.

"Teacher Yun said that, too."

"Teacher Yun? Really?"

Everyone's eyes grew bigger.

Among the teachers, Yun Gang-il stood out. He had been to prison after leading a demonstration as a junior in the History Department of Chonnam

다. 이것 아니면 저것이다. 강함, 용기, 아름다움, 존엄성. 이러한 면모들은 두 집단이 갖고 있는 성격—적이 분명한—으로 이 선택은 사회의 어느 계급보다 용이하다, 라고 윤강일은 말했었다. 그가 잘 쓰는 용어들은 다음과 같다.

혁명. 비지. 피티. 전사. 빨치산. 무장투쟁. 계급투쟁. 시가전. 유격전. 죽창. 게릴라. 봉기. 제국주의. 자본주의. 주변부 자본주의. 종속이론. 해방신학. 제3세계. 민중. 프랑스 혁명. 파리코뮌. 러시아 혁명. 레닌. 볼셰비키. 베트남. 통일…… 이런 용어들은 잠시 동안 역사 한가운데에 젖게 하는 마력을 갖고 있었다. 그러나 어떤 역사인가. 전봉준의 농민전쟁. 항일 유격대. 이름 없이 죽어간 전사들이 만들어낸 역사와 어떻게 관통할 수 있는가.

윤강일은 운동권 지도부 중의 한 사람이었다.

모두들 의아한 듯이 형자를 쳐다보고 있었다. 철순이가 참지 못하고 물었다.

"언니, 자세히 말해봐. 윤 선생님이 정말 그랬다는 거야?"

그중 나이가 많아 형자를 언니라고 불렀다. 형자가 고개를 끄덕였다. 영순이가 말했다.

"정말 믿기지 않아. 아는 것도 많은 분이 어찌 그럴 수

National University. During social gatherings after class, Yun had often talked his prison experience. Hearing him talk so enthusiastically, they had almost wished to go to prison, too.

Yun asked a question, for which he had already prepared an answer:

"You'd think that people would be lonely in prison, away from the outside world, wouldn't you?"

"No. Not at all lonely."

He said that all prisoners were united as a group with a very strong sense of solidarity, no matter how strictly they were isolated from each other. This sense of solidarity penetrated even the very thick walls of the prison. Those walls were alive and speaking: prisoners communicated with each other by banging on them. They could understand each other through a simple word or a glance. Prison could not shut people off from society. Prisoners were a group of people that indicted a society—and a feisty group they were. Those were Yun's words. He added that a group of workers was also feisty. Yun explained the similarity through illustrations.

"Human beings have two sides: strength and weakness, courage and fear, beauty and ugliness,

가 있어? 지는 싸움이라니…… 윤 선생님 지금 어딨어?"

"여기에 없어. 도시를 빠져나갔어."

형자는 자세한 경위를 들려주었다.

형자는 금남로 전투에서 윤강일을 보았고 MBC 앞에서 시위대를 선동하는 그를 보았다. 이마에 끈을 질끈 동여매고 한 손을 휘두르며 구호를 외쳤다. 시민들은 폭력의 정당성을 획득하고 있었다. 공수대원들의 무자비한 학살은 공포 분위기를 넘어, 산다는 것 자체를 뒤흔들어 놓았다. 젊은이들은 숨을 곳도 없었다. 시내에 인접한 동네에서 살고 있는 젊은이들은 가택수색을 피해 변두리 쪽으로 방황하고 있었다. 그곳에도 이미 계엄군으로 무장되어 있었다. 결국 죽음 아니면 싸움이었다. 인간의 존엄성이 파괴된 데서 나오는 근원적 폭력성이 폭발되어갔다.

형자는 시위대들과 섞이어 목이 터져라 외쳤다. 윤강일은 목이 쉬었는지 말소리가 제대로 나오지 않았다. 그는 시위대들과 더불어 불이 붙은 오토바이를 MBC 건물 속으로 밀어붙였다. 몇 번을 더 시도하다가 드디어 MBC는 불길에 휩싸였다. 불빛에 일렁이는 윤강일의 두 눈은 활활 타오르고 있었고 그것은 마치 혁명의 봉홧불을 높이 쳐든

and dignity and baseness. But those two groups aren't allowed to show their duality. Only one side is permitted. It's either this or that. Strength, courage, beauty, and dignity are the obvious characteristics of those two groups, so it's easier for them to choose that side than the other." This was what Yun had said. He used the following terms very often.

"Revolution," "BG," "PT," "fighter," "partisan," "armed struggle," "class struggle," "street fighting," "guerrilla fighting," "bamboo spears," "guerrillas," "revolt," "imperialism," "capitalism," "marginal capitalism," "theory of dependence," "liberation theology," "the third world," "people," "French Revolution," "Paris Commune," "Russian Revolution," "Lenin," "Bolshevik," "Vietnam," "unification"...[3] These words had a magical power to momentarily transport an audience into the middle of history. But what kind of history? A peasant revolution led by Jeon Bong-jun; an anti-Japanese guerrilla unit: How could someone really comprehend history made by anonymous fighters?

Yun was one of the leaders of the pro-democracy movement.

Everyone was casting a doubtful glance towards

자의 눈빛과도 같았다. 형자는 그때 승세는 우리 쪽에 있음을 의심치 않았다. MBC와 인접해 있는 인가에서는 짐보따리를 들고 나오는 사람들로 혼잡을 이루고 있었다. 아이들은 소리쳐 울어댔다. 시위대들은 불길이 번지지 않도록 최선을 다했다. 새벽의 여명이 밝아올 때까지 그들은 목이 터져라 외치며 돌아다녔다. 더 이상 걸어 다닐 힘도 없었을 때에야 그들은 집으로 돌아갈 생각을 했다. 헤어지면서 윤강일이 말했다.

"내일 집으로 와라. 새로운 전략을 세워야 하니까."

이튿날(21일) 형자는 윤강일의 하숙방으로 찾아갔다. 운동권 청년 세 명이 모여 있었다. 한 명은 전대 총학생회 간부였다. 윤강일은 현 정세를 간단히 분석한 뒤 시민들의 움직임을 조직적으로 통제해야 한다는 단안을 내렸다. 갑자기 운동권 청년 하나가 숨차게 들어왔다.

"드디어 놈들이 발포를 시작했어."

모두들 경악했다. 백주의 공식적인 총기 발포는 이제 최후의 결전을 피할 수 없다는 사실을 명백하게 알려주었다.

"평화적 해결은 끝났군." 하면서 윤강일은 초조한 기색을 내보였다. 그들은 도청으로 갔다. 지금까지의 낭만적

Hyeong-ja. Impatient, Cheol-sun asked, "'Eonni, tell us more. Did Teacher Yun really say that?"

They called Hyeong-ja "'Eonni," because she was older.[4] Hyeong-ja nodded. Yeong-sun said, "I cannot believe it. How could anyone as knowledgeable as Teacher Yun have said that? Losing battle? Where is he now?"

"He's not here. He left Gwangju."

Hyeong-ja told them in detail what had happened.

Hyeong-ja saw Yun Gang-il during the Geumnam-ro street fight. She also witnessed him leading demonstrators in front of the MBC building. With a cloth tied around his forehead, he was raising his arms up and down and shouting slogans. This was a time when citizens were justified in responding with violence. The airborne troops' ruthless massacre did not simply sow terror but actually threatened their lives. There was no place for young men even to hide. Those who lived near downtown ran away, wandering around the outskirts of the city to avoid house searches. On the outskirts troops were enforcing martial law. In short, it was fight or die. Violence was a natural response to the destruction of their lives and dignity as human beings.

이고 들떠 있던 분위기가 일시에 사라진 듯했다. 도청 방어선과 시민들 사이에 총을 맞은 시체가 서너 구 쓰러져 있었다. 아직도 죽지 않고 아스팔트 위에서 꿈틀거리고 있는 사람을 구해내려고 뛰어나가는 시민들이 있었다. 적의 조준 사격은 그들 역시 사살해버렸다. 그러고는 연발로 요란하게 위협사격을 가했다. 계엄군 쪽에서 시체의 다리를 잡고 끌고 가기 시작했다. 용감한 시민들이 달려들어 이쪽 편에 가까이 있는 몇 구의 시체를 끌고 왔다. 시민들은 눈물을 흘렸다. 윤강일은 침통한 표정으로 그 광경을 지켜보다가 인파를 헤쳐나갔다. 형자도 따라갔다. 전대 총학생회 간부도 따라갔다. 세 사람은 운동권의 아지트인 사무실로 들어갔다. 윤강일은 계속 침통한 얼굴을 하고 있었다. 학생회 간부가 말했다.

"형, 최후의 결전이 다가오고 있어요."

"그래. 결전이 끝나면 엄청난 검거 선풍이 불 거야."

멀리서 연발의 총성이 들려왔다. 윤강일이 계속해서 말했다.

"총기가 나왔다는 것은 대단히 의미심장한 거야."

"어떻게요?"

형자가 물었다.

Hyeong-ja shouted as loud as she could together with the other demonstrators. Yun seemed to have lost his voice as a result of all his shouting. He was one of the demonstrators who set a motorcycle on fire and pushed it towards the MBC building. After a few attempts, the building was engulfed in flames. In the flaring light of the fire, Yun's eyes were also blazing. They looked like the eyes of someone lifting up the beacon of revolution. At that moment, Hyeong-ja didn't doubt that they were winning. Streets around the MBC building were crowded with people who had escaped their houses, carrying bundles in their hands. Babies were crying. Demonstrators tried their best to prevent the fire from spreading. They walked around until dawn, shouting and chanting slogans. When they remembered that they should perhaps go home, they realized they didn't have any strength left—not even to walk. When they were parting, Yun told her, "Come to my house tomorrow. We'll have to think about strategies."

The next day, May twenty-first, Hyeong-ja went to Yun's boarding house. Three young activists greeted her. One was a leader of the Chonnam National University student government. Yun presented a

"피를 보면 피를 부르게 마련이지. 어차피 지는 싸움일 텐데, 얼마나 피를 흘려야 할까."

"지는 싸움이라뇨?"

형자는 그의 말을 이해할 수 없었다. 싸움의 양상은 점점 더 격렬해지고 시민들은 하나같이 투쟁에 나서고 있지 않은가.

"총기가 나왔다는 것이 바로 그거야. 힘의 대결은 비정한 거야. 4·19의 총기 발사하곤 다르지. 그때는 장소가 서울이야. 이런 싸움이 서울에서 벌어졌다면 이 정권은 가는 거야. 그러나 여기는 소도시야. 몇 군데만 차단하면 꼼짝없이 갇혀버리게 돼. 결국 엄청난 희생만 치르게 되겠지."

윤강일이 말을 멈추었다. 잠시 후에 다시 말하는 그의 목소리가 돌같이 굳어 있었다.

"이럴 때 무모하게 피를 흘리는 것보다 일보 후퇴의 전략을 세우는 것도 현명한 거야."

"형, 아무래도 일단 피신해야겠어요."

"나도 그 생각이야. 사태를 관망하면서 새로운 전의를 가다듬어야지."

"어떻게 그럴 수가 있어요?"

brief analysis of the current situation and concluded that they had to systematically control people's movements. Suddenly an activist rushed in and said, "They've begun firing."

They were all completely shocked. If the military had opened fire in broad daylight, clearly they could no longer avoid a life-and-death confrontation.

"Peaceful resolution is impossible now."

As Yun said that, he looked nervous. They went to the governor's office building complex together. The romantic and somewhat thrilling atmosphere seemed to have evaporated in an instant. On the ground between the line of defense at the complex and the crowds of citizens were the bodies of several people who had been shot. A few people darted towards those who were still alive and writhing to try to help. The military aimed at them and fired, killing them with precision. Then they fired successive loud warning shots. The troops enforcing martial law began dragging bodies away by their legs. A few brave citizens dashed towards the nearest bodies, dragging them to their side. People cried. Yun observed the scene with a grave and somber expression and then made his way out through the

형자가 분노를 띤 목소리로 말했다.

"선생님들이 말하던 시가전, 봉기 등등이 나오고 있는데……"

"상황을 정확히 볼 줄 알아야 돼."

윤강일은 두 사람을 번갈아 보며 단안을 내리듯 말하였다.

"어쨌든 이 도시를 빠져나가자."

"그래요 형. 조금도 지체할 수 없어요."

그들은 다급하게 일어섰다. 형자가 소리쳤다.

"가면 안 돼요."

밖으로 나가는 그들을 따라가며 형자가 다시 외쳤다.

"가면 안 돼요. 우리가 이기고 있잖아요."

윤강일이 뒤를 돌아다보았다. 연발총 소리가 다시 들려왔다. 그의 눈빛이 흔들렸다. 그가 한 발을 내디디면서 말했다.

"어차피 지는 싸움이야. 너도 같이 가자."

"싫어요." 하면서 형자는 층계 난간을 꽉 붙들고 그들이 빠져나가는 것을 노려보았다. 배신감이 치밀어 올랐다. 그녀는 도청 쪽으로 달려갔다. 각종 총기로 무장한 수백 명의 시위대들이 도청 앞으로 진격하여 치열한 총격전

crowd. Hyeong-ja followed him. The Chonnam University Student Government leader followed them, too. The three went to an office, an activist hideout. Yun still wore a sad expression. The student leader said, "Hyeong, the life-and-death battle is here."[5)]

"Right. And after the battle, there will be a sweeping round-up."

They could hear the sound of firing in rapid succession. Yun continued, "The use of firearms is very significant."

"How?" asked Hyeong-ja.

"Blood calls for blood. This is going to be a losing battle. I wonder how much blood we should shed."

"A losing battle?"

Hyeong ja couldn't understand it. The fight was becoming more violent and all citizens were participating, so why would they lose?

"Because of the firearms. A physical battle will be merciless. This is different from the firing during the April 19th Student Revolution. That happened in Seoul. If this happened in Seoul, the current regime would be over. But this is a small city. If they block off a few roads, we'll be isolated and have no way out. In the end, there will only be enormous sacri-

을 벌이고 있었다. 그녀는 야학에 잠깐 얼굴을 비추다 만 소년을 보았다. 구두닦이였다. 소년은 카빈총을 들고 싸우고 있었다. 소년이 형자를 기억하고 씩 웃었다. 그리고 카빈총을 높이 치켜들어 보였다. 형자는 총을 든 사람들을 본능적으로 알아보았다. 대부분이 그녀와 같은 하층계급 사람들이었다. 그녀는 그들과 같이 저녁 늦게 해방의 기쁨을 나누었다. 개인은 개인을 열어, 마을은 마을을 열어, 거리는 거리를 열어, 금남로는 금남로를 열어, 최후의 결전장인 도청의 열림과 더불어 민주 공동체를 이루어냈던 것이다.

말을 마치고 형자는 한 사람 한 사람 둘러보았다. 모두들 충격을 받은 듯 멍하니 앉아 있었다. 형자가 말했다.

"그건 그거구, 이제부터 일을 찾아보기로 하자."

형자는 야학생 중에서 남다른 데가 있었다. 야학에 나오긴 했지만 학과 공부를 하러 나오지는 않았고 이곳에 모이는 여러 공장의 근로자들을 만나기 위해서였다. 형자는 남의 이야기를 잘 들어주었다. 공장에서 일어나는 일이며 집안 얘기, 또는 애태우는 연애 얘기까지 들어주었다. 순분이가 전태일이며 석정남이라는 이름을 알게 된

fices."

Yun Gang-il paused. When he resumed a little later, his voice was as hard as a rock.

"The wise thing to do is to adopt a strategy of retreat rather than shed blood recklessly."

"Hyeong, we should first escape," said the student leader.

"That's what I am thinking. We should keep an eye on the situation and prepare for a future fight," was Yun's response.

"How could you?" Hyeong-ja said in an angry voice. "This is the very situation of a street fight, revolt, etc., that you teachers have always been talking about..."

"You have to assess the situation accurately," Yun concluded looking from one to the other and said, "Let's get out of this city, at any rate."

"Yes, Hyeong. We should not linger any longer."

They hurriedly stood up. Hyeong-ja shouted at them, "No, you mustn't go."

Following them out, Hyeong-ja shouted again, "You mustn't go. We're winning."

Yun turned around. They could all hear the sound of rapid firing again. Yun's eyes wavered for a second. Stepping forward, he said, "This is a losing bat-

것도 형자 덕분이었다. 형자는 겉장이 다 닳은 잡지책을 갖고 왔다. 『대화』지였다. '불타는 눈물'이 어찌 석정남 하나뿐이겠는가.

"언니, 이런 글이라면 우리도 쓸 수 있겠네." 하고 순분이는 말했다.

"글이란 게 별게 아니야. 혼자서 간직하기엔 너무 벅찬 것 있잖니? 또 공장에서 일하다보면 화나는 일들이 많잖아. 그런 일들을 글로 쓰면 되는 거지."

"그래두 글재주가 있어야지."

형자는 도서 목록 중에서 책 한 권을 꺼내 보였다. 순분이는 페이지를 넘겨보았지만 너무 어려웠다.

"뭐가 뭔지 모르겠네. 언니, 우리 얘기를 이상하게 써놓았잖아. 우리 얘긴 우리가 써야 되지 않을까?"

그래서 그녀들은 작은 책자를 만들었다. 시도 있었고 수기, 고향으로 보내는 편지, 수필 등등이 실렸다. 형자의 의견으로 이름을 모두 뗴었다.

"이름을 떼고 읽어봐. 모두가 우리들 글 같잖아."

정말 그랬다. 모두 각자가 쓴 것 같았다. 하나하나 읽을 때는 잘 드러나지 않는데 전체적으로 읽고 나면 치밀어 오르는 것이 있었다. 개인의 불만들이 합쳐져서 집단의

tle. Join us."

"No."

Firmly holding the balustrade of the stairs, she stared fiercely at them as they disappeared. She felt betrayed. She ran towards the governor's office. Hundreds of demonstrators, armed with various firearms, had advanced close to the building and were exchanging shots. She saw a boy who briefly attended night school. He was a shoeshine boy. He was fighting with a carbine in his hand. He remembered her and smiled. Then, he raised his carbine high. Hyeong-ja could instinctively recognize the people with guns. They were mostly lower class people like her. She shared the joy of liberation with them later that evening. Individuals, neighborhoods, streets, and Geumnam-ro street all opened up to create a democratic community together with the opening of the governor's office building complex, the site of their last decisive battle.

After finishing her story, Hyeong-ja looked around at her friends one by one. They all looked dumbfounded and shocked. Hyeong-ja said, "Well, that's that. Now let's figure out what we can do."

Hyeong-ja was a little different from the other

분노가 표현되었다. 순분으로서는 처음으로 자신을 되돌아보는 계기가 되었다. 그녀 가정의 가난만 탓해왔는데 그게 아니었다. 집단의 문제였다. 노동자 집단의.

"아주 간단하게 생각해봐." 하고 형자는 말했다.

"우린 뼈 빠지게 일하잖아. 일한 만큼 대가를 받아야지. 이건 권리야. 그런데 우린 권리를 빼앗겼어. 다시 찾아야 될 텐데 순순히 찾을 수가 없거든. 혼자서는 너무 약해. 하지만 힘을 합치면 강해지지."

형자는 노조의 필요성을 강조했다. 그녀는 노조라고 발음할 땐 꼭 앞에 '민주'자를 붙였다. 민주노조, 기실 노조라면 알고 있었지만 기업주 편이라서 심드렁하게 생각하고 있었다.

강학들과 맞서서 이야기를 주고받을 수 있는 야학생은 형자뿐이었다. 야학생들은 강학들에게 고마움을 느끼고 있었지만 형자만은 그렇지 않았다. 강학들은 그나마 야학에 와서 근로자들을 접함으로써 올바르게 살 수 있는 지침을 배운다는 것이었다. 어느 때인가 강학들이 노학연대의 필요성을 강조했다.

"정말 노학연대를 말하고 싶으면 최소한 3년 이상 근로자 생활을 해야만 돼요." 하고 형자는 주장했다. 이 말에

night school students. Although she attended the school, she wasn't really there to study, but to meet workers from other factories. She was a very good listener. She listened to other people's stories about their factories, families, and even anxious love lives. It was also thanks to Hyeong-ja that Sunbun got to know such names as Jeon Tae-il and Seok Jeong-nam.[6] Hyeong-ja once brought a magazine with a tattered cover called "Dialogue" to the school. Seok Jeong-nam wasn't the only laborer shedding "burning tears."[7]

"Eonni, we could write something like this, too," said Sunbun at the time.

"There's nothing special about writing, you know. There are some things that we just have to get off our chest, right? Also, there are many things that upset us in our factories, aren't there? We can just write about them."

"You still need talent, don't you?"

Hyeong-ja took out one of the books on their reading list. Sunbun took a look at it, but it was too difficult.

"I can't understand, Eonni. It talks about our stories in strange language. Perhaps, we should write our stories..."

63

강학들은 선험적 경험이라는 것도 있다고 맞섰다. 형자가
말했다.

"대학생들이 노동 현장에 뛰어드는 것은 훌륭하다고 봐
요. 그들은 공부한 이론을 현장에 적용하려고 안달을 하
지요. 최소한 대학생들이 노동 현장에 들어올 때는 이론
적으로 통일이 되어야 합니다. 이론은 이론이 갖는 성격
으로 분열이 일어나게 마련이어서 각자 분파가 생겨나지
요. 근로자는 이리 쏠리고 저리 쏠리다가 방향감각을 잃
게 되고 주체적으로 설 수도 없게 돼요. 그러니까 개인의
선택에 의해서 노동 현장에 들어올 것이 아니라 통합된
조직과 이론을 갖고 집단적 차원에서 들어와야지요. 아니
면 아예 들어올 생각도 하지 않는 게 좋아요. 우리는 우리
가 갖고 있는 성격으로도 자연히 전투적이 될 수밖에 없
으니까요."

이러한 말에 강학들은 아무 대답도 하지 못했다. 유식
한 강학들이 쩔쩔매는 것이 순분으로서는 기분이 좋았다.
순분네 공장에도 여대생 두 명이 신분을 감추고 들어와서
는―나중에 알았지만―몇 달 동안 열심히 일한 적이 있었
다. 단발머리에 운동화를 신고 옷차림도 털털해서 그녀들
이 여대생이라고는 아무도 몰랐다. 그녀들은 노조 결성의

So they created a small book. It included poems, memoirs, letters to their families in their home-towns, and essays. At Hyeong-ja's suggestion, they published their writings anonymously.

"Read without names! They all seem as if any of us could have written them."

That was true. All the writings seemed to have been written by each and every one of them. Something emerged from the entire book—something that wasn't clear when they were reading the individual pieces. Read together, individual dissatisfaction became group dissatisfaction. It was the first opportunity for Sunbun to reflect on her life. She had been blaming her family's poverty for whatever happened to her, but that was not the problem. It was the problem of a group—the whole group of workers.

"It's actually quite simple," said Hyeong-ja. "We are working our fingers to the bone. We must be compensated accordingly. That's our right. But our rights are taken away from us. So we have to regain them. We just cannot get them back without strug-gling for them. An individual is not strong enough. However, if we combine our strength, we become stronger."

필요성을 강조했다. 그런데 과정에서 문제가 생겼다. 한 여대생은 노조를 결성하기 전에 의식화를 위한 소모임을 주장했고, 딴 여대생은 노조 결성을 먼저 해놓고 투쟁을 벌이면 자연히 의식화가 된다는 것이었다. 근로자들은 이 말도 맞고 저 말도 맞는 것 같아 이리 왔다 저리 갔다 하다가 결국은 회사 간부들이 알게 되어 그녀들은 쫓겨나게 되었다. 몇 명의 근로자들도 쫓겨나게 되었다. 여대생들은 그들 세계로 갈 곳이 있었지만 쫓겨난 근로자들은 갈 곳도 없었다. 블랙리스트에 올라 어느 곳에도 취업할 수가 없었다.

형자는 자신에 대해서 아무 말도 안 했지만 어려서부터 서울 모 방직 회사에 다녔고 임금 투쟁으로 해고 근로자가 되었다가 본래 고향인 이곳에 내려온 것으로 소문이 나돌았다.

층계 오르는 발자국 소리가 들렸다. 미숙이가 일어나 문을 열었다. 영철이었다. 같은 야학생으로 자개공이었다.

"혹시나 해서 들렀어."

"이제야 나타나?"

Hyeong-ja emphasized the need for a union. Whenever she mentioned the word "union," she always prefaced it with "democratic." A democratic union. In fact, there was an existing the union, but they didn't pay much attention to it, because it was working for the employer.

Hyeong-ja was the only student at night school who could engage as an equal in discussions with the teachers. Although most students were simply grateful to their teachers, Hyeong-ja had a slightly different attitude. She claimed that the teachers were learning to live an upright life thanks to workers at the night school. When teachers once insisted on solidarity between laborers and students, Hyeong-ja argued, "If you really want to discuss solidarity between laborers and students, you have to work as a laborer for at least three years before you can even bring up the subject." Teachers countered with the argument that there was such a thing as transcendental cognition. Hyeong-ja responded,

"I think it's honorable for college students to throw themselves into the labor scene. They are anxious to apply the theories they have learned to real life. When college students enter factories, though, I think they should at least be unified about

미숙이가 핀잔을 주었다. 영철은 머리를 긁적였다. 영
순이가 말했다.

"지금 우리가 겪은 이야기를 하고 있던 중이야. 너도 얘
기해봐."

형자가 고개를 저으며 말을 막았다.

"이제 겪은 얘기는 그만 하자. 지금 중요한 건 그게 아
니야. 지금부터가 정말 중요한 거야."

형자의 말로는 완전한 해방이 아니라는 것이다. 지금
광주는 해방구이지만 고립된 해방구다. 해방구라는 말 자
체가 풍기는 구역 분계선이 있다. 이제부터는 해방구를
중심으로 구역 분계선을 넓혀 나가야 한다. 전라도 전역,
경상남북도, 충청남북도, 강원도, 경기도, 서울이어야 한
다. 그리고 한라에서 백두까지 해방구가 되어야만 진정한
해방이다. 이어서 형자가 말했다.

"……그러려면 투쟁에 적극적으로 가담해야 돼."

"난 총을 들고 싶어."

영순이의 말을 미숙이가 받았다.

"난 시민군으로 들어갈 거야."

"여자도 시민군이 있대?"

영철이가 놀렸다. 미숙이가 눈을 흘기며 말했다.

their theories. Because theories are theories, they are bound to sow dissention and generate factions among the laborers. Laborers lean to this or that faction and eventually lose their own sense of direction and ability to stand independently. So college students shouldn't join the labor scene as individuals but as members of an organization with a unified structure and theory. If not, they shouldn't even think about joining. Laborers can't help becoming feisty anyway, because we are who we are."

No teacher could counter her argument. It was satisfying for Sunbun to see intelligent teachers unable to respond. Once two female college students came to work incognito at Sunbun's factory—she only found out later that they were students—and worked very hard for a few months. Nobody suspected they were college students because of their humble appearance—bobbed hair, sneakers, and unassuming clothes. They enthusiastically argued that the workers needed a union. However, the process of establishing a union wasn't smooth. One student insisted that they needed to organize small groups for consciousness-raising of the workers before they formed a union, while the other claimed that laborers could naturally acquire consciousness,

"여잔 시민군이 못 되나 뭐."

"총을 쏠 줄 알아야지."

"배우면 되지."

여러 제안이 나왔지만 딱히 결정을 볼 수가 없었다. 상황을 알고 나서 정하기로 하고, 원칙은 도청으로 들어간다는 것이었다. 아무도 이의를 제기하는 사람이 없었다.

도청 분수대 앞에 도착했을 때 막 허수아비에 불이 붙여지고 있었다. 붉은 글씨로 ×××살인마라고 쓰여 있었다. 군중들은 돌을 던지며 "빨리 죽여라" 하고 발을 굴렀다. 허수아비의 발끝에서부터 불이 붙어 삽시간에 온몸이 타오르자 군중들은 열광적으로 환호했다.

그녀들은 도청 정문으로 갔다. 정문에는 '수습대책위원회'라고 쓰여 있는 띠를 어깨에 두른 청년들이 일일이 출입을 통제하고 있었다. 형자가 나서서 말했다.

"우리도 할 일이 있을 것 같은데요. 들여보내 주세요."

"안 됩니다."

몇 번 사정을 해보았지만 완강하게 거절당했다. 그녀들은 낙심해서 한동안 우두커니 서 있었다. 사망자를 확인하기 위해 들어가는 사람들은 출입이 허용되고 있었다.

once they established a union and began to lead the fight. Workers were confused because both arguments sounded right, so they wavered. While they were wavering, the managers of the company found out about the two students and immediately fired them. A few laborers were fired as well. Whereas the students could return to their own world, the laborers couldn't. They couldn't get a job in any other company either because they were blacklisted.

Although Hyeong-ja didn't talk about it herself, rumor had it that she returned to her hometown after being fired from a textile company in Seoul, where she had been involved in a wage struggle.

They could hear footsteps coming up the stairs. Misuk got up and opened the door. It was Yeong-cheol. A classmate at the night school, Yeong-cheol was a shell worker at a mother-of-pearl workshop.

"I decided to drop by just in case..."

"You couldn't have come any later?"

Misuk mildly rebuked him. Yeong-cheol scratched his head. Yeong-sun said, "We've been talking about what we went through. Tell us what happened to you."

미숙이는 오빠 생각이 나서 한번 사정해볼까 하다가 혼자서는 들어갈 마음이 나지 않았다. Y라는 완장을 두른 사람도 출입이 허용되었다. 영철은 무슨 생각이 떠올랐는지 "잠깐만 기다려" 하고 급히 뛰어갔다. 얼마 후에 다시 나타난 영철의 손에 Y자가 쓰인 완장이 다섯 개 들려 있었다.

"이걸 차고 들어가. 난 YWCA에 가야겠어. 그곳에 용준이 형이 「투사회보」를 만들고 있어. 나보고 등사를 도와달라고 해서 그러마고 했지."

용준이라면 '들불야학' 팀의 중심인물이었다. 그녀들은 완장을 두르고 정문 앞에 다가갔다. 아무 말 없이 들여보내 주었다.

2

도청 안마당 한구석에 시체들이 놓여 있었다. 대부분의 시체는 이미 그 형상을 제대로 알아볼 수가 없었다. 총상을 입거나 곤봉을 맞은 시체는 머리와 얼굴이 짓뭉개져 있었고, 대검으로 난자된 시체는 붓거나 부패해 냄새가 진동했다. 눈알이 튀어나온 시체, 팔이 떨어져 나간 시체,

Shaking her head sideways, Hyeong-ja interrupted: "Let's stop talking about the past. That's not that important now. What will happen from now on is what really matters."

According to Hyeong-ja, this wasn't complete liberation. "Gwangju is now liberated, but isolated. As the name 'liberated area' suggests, it's a separate area. From now on, we have to expand this liberated area. It should include the entire area of Jeolla-do, Gyeongsangnambuk-do, Chungchongnambuk-do, Gangwon-do, Gyeonggi-do, and Seoul. Only when the entire country, from Halla to Baekdu, is liberated, will we have true liberation." Then Hyeong-ja said, "For that to happen, we have to actively participate in the struggle."

"I want arms."

In response to this remark by Yeong-sun, Misuk said, "I'm going to join the citizen's army."

"A woman citizen soldier?" Yeong-cheol teased. Scowling at him, Misuk said, "Why, can't a woman become a soldier?"

"You must know how to shoot a gun."

"I can learn."

Although they came up with many ideas, they couldn't decide what to do. They agreed to the

목이 잘려서 몸과 분리된 시체, 유방이 잘렸는지 가슴께
가 너덜너덜한 여학생도 있었다. 혹시 오빠가 있나, 일일
이 시체들을 확인하던 미숙이와 동료들은 스스로 놀라 손
이나 손수건으로 입을 막았다. 오열을 하다가 그대로 기
절해버린 부인들도 있었다. 미숙이 오빠는 없었다. 그녀
들은 '작전상황실'이라고 써 붙인 곳으로 갔다. 총을 어깨
에 멘 남자가 물었다.

"어떻게 오셨습니까?"

"우리도 도청을 지키려고 왔어요. 무슨 일을 하면 좋을
까요?"

형자가 말했다.

"글쎄요. 지금 무기 반납 문제로 싸우고들 있느라 정신
이 없어요. 댁들이 알아서 필요한 부서를 찾아보도록 하
세요."

그녀들은 상황실을 나와 이 층으로 올라갔다. 총을 메
고 바쁜 듯이 걸어다니는 남자들 속에서 그녀들은 갈팡질
팡했다. 어디 한군데 제대로 자리 잡힌 곳이 없었다. 마침
내 그녀들은 '취사실'이라고 쓰인 커다란 사무실을 찾아
냈다. 그곳에 삽십여 명의 여자들이 저녁 준비를 하고 있
었다. 여학생과 근로자들이 대부분이었다. 형자는 그중

principle that they should occupy the governor's office. They would make a decision after checking the situation. Nobody objected.

When they arrived at the plaza near the fountain in front of the governor's office building complex, they encountered crowds setting fire to an effigy. "XXX, Devilish Murderer" was written on it in red ink. Crowds were throwing rocks at it, while stamping and crying, "Hurry up! Kill him!" With its feet set on fire, the effigy was engulfed in flames in an instant amidst cheering crowds.

They went to the main gate, where young men wearing shoulder bands that said "Committee for the Control of the Situation" were monitoring people's comings and goings. Hyeong-ja approached and said, "We'd like to work, too. Please let us in."

"No."

Although they reiterated their plea, they were repeatedly denied access to the building. Discouraged, they were at a loss for a while. People who wanted to identify their dead relatives were allowed to enter. Remembering her brother, Misuk thought of pleading again, but realized that she didn't want to enter by herself. People with arm-

몇은 안면이 있는지 손을 맞잡고 인사를 나누었다. 형자 팀들은 자연스럽게 섞여 식사 준비를 했다. 식사 시간은 대중이 없어 자정까지 계속되었다. 형자는 설거지를 끝내고 각 분대실을 찾아가 보았다. 무기 반납 문제를 놓고 강경파와 온건파가 열띠게 논쟁하고 있었다. 강경파들은 대개 룸펜 계층이나 노동자들이었다.

"무기를 반납하자는 놈들은 배신자와 같은 거요."

한 노동자가 총대를 책상 모서리에 탁탁 부딪치며 말했다. 대학생들로 이루어진 '학생수습대책위원회'들은 온건파였다. 그들 중 한 명이 말을 받았다.

"당신들은 또 피를 흘리길 원하는 거요?"

"누가 피를 흘리자고 했소? 피 흘린 것을 헛되이 하지 말자는 말이죠."

강경파.

"무기를 갖고 있는 한 피는 흘리게 마련이오."

온건파.

"무기를 내놓는다고 적들이 우릴 그냥 놔둘 것 같아요. 우린 적을 안 믿어요. 적은 적입니다."

강경파.

"이런 식으로 대치하는 한 수습이란 있을 수 없습니

bands with the letter Y were also granted access. Noticing this, Yeong-cheol ran after them, saying, "Wait a minute." Yeong-cheol soon reappeared with five armbands with the letter Y.

"Take them and go in. I have to go back to the YWCA building. Yong-jun is working on *Fighter's Newsletter* there. He asked me to help him with mimeographing and I said yes."

Yong-jun was one of the leaders of Wildfire Night School. They put on armbands and approached the main gate. This time they were allowed to enter without any objection.

2

There were bodies in a corner of the courtyard. Most were already unrecognizable. Bodies that had been shot or beaten had crushed heads and faces, and those stabbed by bayonets were swollen, rotten, and giving off a stench. There were bodies with protruding eyeballs, bodies separated from heads, and female students whose chest areas were shredded probably because their breasts were stabbed. Misuk and her friends, who were checking bodies one by one, looking for Misuk's brother, were cov-

다."

온건파.

"수습 수습, 자꾸 그러는데 그 말이 뭔 말이오? 도청을
내놓자는 말 아니오? 어떻게 찾은 도청인데……"

강경파.

"무기를 반납하면서 우리에게 유리한 고지를 따내면 되
지 않습니까."

온건파.

온건파들이 말하는 유리한 고지란 구속된 모든 사람을
석방할 것이며, 보상 계획 수립과 치료 대책 완비, 비무장
민간인의 시외 통행, 사실 보도에 노력할 것, 폭도나 불순
분자라는 용어 사용 중지, 사태 수습 후 보복 금지 약속
등등이었다. 이러한 수습안은 강경파들에게 더 심한 반발
을 일으켰다. 한 노동자는 주먹을 쥐어 보이면서 목청을
높였다.

"그건 원점으로 되돌아가자는 것이오. 이미 전쟁은 벌
어졌고 그것도 적들이 먼저 벌인 것인데 왜 우리가 타협
을 해야 합니까? 우린 절대로 항복 안 해요."

"그게 어째 항복입니까? 최후의 타협이지."

온건파.

ering their mouths with their hands or handkerchiefs in shock. There were wives who had passed out, sobbing and crying. They couldn't find Misuk's brother. They went to the office with the sign, "Field Operation Office." A man with a rifle on his shoulder asked, "May I help you?"

"We came to help guard the governor's office building complex. What can we do?" said Hyeong-ja.

"Well, they are busy arguing whether we should turn in our arms or not. Please find a place where you can be helpful."

They went to the second floor. They didn't know what to do among all the men dashing here and darting there with rifles on their shoulders. There wasn't a single place where things looked organized. Finally, they arrived at a big office with the sign "Kitchen." About thirty women were preparing dinner. Most were students and laborers. Hyeong-ja appeared to recognize a few acquaintances, as she was greeting and holding hands with them. They joined the group, as expected, and helped prepare dinner. There wasn't a specific time for dinner, so it lasted until midnight. After finishing the dishes, Hyeong-ja dropped by various offices. Hardliners

"항복 아니면 승리지, 왜 그리 머리를 굴려요. 먹물들은 어쩔 수 없다니까."

강경파.

"그럼 무대뽀로 싸우자는 말인데, 전쟁 중에도 전략이라는 게 있지 않습니까?"

온건파.

"전략이라고 세운 것이 겨우 수습이나 하자는 거요? 전쟁 중에 적과 타협하자는 것은 스파이나 하는 짓이오."

강경파.

"스파이라니? 그럼 우리가 스파이란 말이오?"

온건파.

"결국은 스파이 짓과 같은 것이지요."

강경파.

그때 수습위원장이 나섰다.

"당신들 지금까지 신분증 조사를 안 했는데 신분증을 제시하시오."

강경파들의 얼굴이 일그러졌다. 한 노동자가 주민등록증을 내밀었다.

"여기 있다. 똑똑히 봐. 대한민국 정부에서 발행한 거다."

and moderates were having heated arguments over whether to turn in their weapons. The hardliners were mostly workers or unemployed men.

"Those who argue that we should give up our weapons are traitors," said a worker, hitting a corner of a table with the barrel of his rifle. The Students' Committee for the Control of the Situation, composed of college students, were the moderates. One of them responded, "Do you want more bloodshed?"

"Who wants more bloodshed? What I'm saying is that the bloodshed that already occurred shouldn't have been in vain," said a hardliner.

"As long as we have weapons, we're bound to shed blood," responded a moderate.

"Do you think our enemy will leave us alone, even if we give up our arms? We don't trust our enemy. An enemy is an enemy," said a hardliner.

"If we confront them like this, there will never be any resolution," responded a moderate.

"Resolution, resolution—what do you mean by resolution? Isn't that saying we should surrender the governor's office? Do you remember what it took to win it...?" asked a hardliner.

"It would work if we gave up our weapons in

반말이 나오기 시작했다. 강경파들 중에 총대를 움켜쥐는 자들도 있었다. 수습위원장이 말했다.

"이건 보통 신분증이잖소? 이걸 갖고 어떻게 당신 신분을 정확히 알 수 있겠소?"

"대학생이면 다냐? 이 개새끼들아."

턱에 칼자국이 있는 남자가 앞으로 뛰쳐나오며 외쳤다.

"그래 우린 놈팽이다. 놈팽이는 내 땅을 지킬 권리도 없단 말이냐? 너희들만 나라를 생각하는 줄 알아?"

남자가 갑자기 허리에 찬 권총을 뽑아들고 공포를 쏘았다. 수습위원들의 얼굴이 하얗게 질리었다. 그들은 서로 눈짓을 주고받더니 하나 둘씩 빠져나갔다. 나가는 위원들 중의 한 명이 옆사람에게 소곤거렸다.

"무식한 놈들하곤 말도 안 통한다니까."

나가는 위원들을 향하여 다시 한 번 공포를 쏘며 한 남자가 외쳤다.

"무기 반납 어쩌구 또 떠들면 대갈통에 총구멍을 뚫어놓을 테다."

적들은 무기로 무장돼 있는데 왜 무기를 내놓자는 말인가, 칼에는 칼, 무기엔 무기. 지금의 무기는 바로 우리의 목숨이지 않은가. 강경파들만이 남았을 때 아무 논란이

exchange for something to our advantage, wouldn't it?" said a moderate.

Then the moderates explained that by "something to our advantage" they meant releasing the arrested, establishing plans for the treatment of the wounded and reparations for the dead and wounded, allowing unarmed civilians to pass in and out of the city, making an effort for truthful reporting, stopping using terms like "mobs" and "rebellious elements," and promising not to retaliate after the situation is settled. Hardliners became even more upset at this proposal. A laborer made a fist and shouted, "That's going back to the starting point. The war has already broken out, and at the enemy's initiative for that matter, so why should we compromise? We'll never capitulate."

"Why is it capitulation? It's the final compromise," said a moderate.

"It's either capitulation or victory. Why are you racking your brain like that? There's no help for the educated, is there?" said a hardliner.

"So you're saying that we should fight no matter what. Don't you need strategies even during a war?" asked a moderate.

"Controlling the situation is what you came up

없었다. 그들은 자랑스레 총을 만지기도 하고, 먹물들을 보기 좋게 한 방 먹인 것에 대해 즐거워하기도 했다. 형자가 한 남자를 붙들고 말했다.

"우리끼리 지도부를 만들면 되겠네요. 그래서 우리가 주체적으로 도청을 장악하고 일을 해나가면 되잖아요."

"지도부라뇨?"

남자가 의아한 듯 형자를 쳐다보았다.

"일을 해나가려면 조직이 필요하잖아요. 마치 노조를 만들듯이 말예요."

"여기가 공장인가요?"

"말하자면 강력한 조직이 필요하다는 말이지요."

형자는 안타까워 말이 잘 나오지 않았다. 남자가 말했다.

"지도부라는 건 먹물들이나 하는 거 아녜요? 학생수습 위원인가 뭔가 하는 치들이 도청에 들어와서 제일 먼저 한 것이 지도부를 만든 겁니다."

"글쎄 그건 잘못된 지도부고요. 정말 강경파들이 지도부를 이루어야 한단 말예요."

"글쎄, 그런 생각은 해보지 않았어요."

딴 사람을 붙들고 말해봐도 역시 같은 대답이었다. 의

with for a strategy? Proposing to compromise with the enemy during war is what a spy does," said a hardliner.

"Spy? Are you saying we're spies?" asked a moderate.

"In the end, what you're arguing for isn't that different from what a spy does," said a hardliner.

At that point, the committee chair stepped forward, saying, "We haven't checked your IDs yet. Please present your IDs."

Hardliners frowned. A laborer stuck out his resident registration card.

"Here it is. Look at it carefully. It was issued by the Korean government."

People began using the impolite form of speech. A few clutched their rifles tightly. The committee chair asked, "This is just a regular ID, isn't it? How can we know who you are by this?"

"You think being a college student is everything? Sons-of-bitches!"

A man with a knife scar on his chin rushed forward and shouted, "Right, we're bums! Are you saying a bum doesn't have the right to defend his country? Do you think you're the only ones who care about our country?"

기로움과 공분으로 도청을 지키고는 있었지만 집단을 이루어 강력한 지도부를 이루기엔 너무나 힘이 미약했다. 조직이 아니라 개개인으로 도청에 들어온 때문이기도 했다. 그들은 지도부를 만들 생각은 않고 각기 제 위치로 돌아갔다. 형자는 취사실로 돌아와서 한숨도 자지 못했다. 그녀는 이상한 생각이 들었다. 생각해보니 운동권 청년들은 거의 보지 못했던 것이다. 형자는 윤강일에 의해 운동권 청년들과 여러 번 접촉한 적이 있었다. 기본적으로는 노학연대를 반대하는 입장이었지만 지역사회인만큼 완전히 배제하기는 힘든 일이었다. 운동권 내에서는 민청 세력이 지도부를 형성하고 있었다. 아직 운동 논리도 없고 선배도 없고 사회과학적 지식도 없었던 1974년, 몇백 명의 대학생들은 의분과 유신 독재에의 항거로 학생운동의 기치를 내걸었다. 그들이 운동권의 지도부를 형성한 것은 당연한 일이었다. 여기에 70년대 후반에 들어서면서 재야 인사와 JOC, 민청 세대의 모임인 현대문화연구소, 야학 팀, 구속자 옥바라지 팀인 송백회, 그리고 노동자들이 조심스럽게 연대를 맺고 있었다. 형자는 처음에는 의구심을 갖고 그들을 바라보았다. 그들과 접촉하면서 차츰 좋은 점을 발견하게 되었다. 운동의 결집점이 단순히 이론이나

Suddenly he took a gun from his belt and fired a blank. The committee members turned pale. They exchanged glances and began leaving the room one by one. A few were whispering among themselves, "It's impossible to discuss anything with these illiterates."

Firing another blank behind them as they left, the man shouted, "If you talk nonsense again like giving up our weapons, I'll blow a hole in your skull."

When our enemy is armed, why should we give up our arms? A knife for a knife, arms for arms. Aren't our arms our lives? Hardliners who remained all agreed. They handled their guns proudly and enjoyed the fact that they had shown up the intellectuals. Hyeong-ja said to a man, "We should create our own leadership. Then, we can take charge of the governor's office building complex and begin to work."

"Leadership?" he looked at Hyeong-ja questioningly.

"We need an organization to work—like making a labor union, you know."

"Is this a factory?"

"I'm saying that we need a strong organization."

Getting somewhat impatient, Hyeong-ja couldn't

사무실이나 기관 운동이 아니라, 인간적인 깊은 신뢰와 도덕적 우위에서 운동의 힘을 모아나가고 있었다. 그렇다고 본능적으로 숨겨져 있는 지식인에 대한 불신을 없애주는 것은 아니었다. 그들의 이론은 들을 만한 부분이었다. 이론적으로 그들은 혁명의 사상을 지녔고, 전사였고, 선진적이었다. 그들이 보통 말하는 무장투쟁, 시가전 등등이 형자의 일상생활을 파고든 것은 숨길 수 없는 사실이었다. 그들에 대한 배신감은 윤강일의 도피로 이미 맛보았지만 역시 지금도 배신감이 치밀어 올랐다. 그렇다면 그녀의 내밀한 한 부분은 그들을 신뢰하고 있었단 말인가. 그 생각에 미치자 형자는 자리에서 벌떡 일어났다. 그리고 꼬부라져 잠들어 있는 동료들을 바라보았다. 저들은 누구인가. 지식도 없고, 이론도 없고, 운동 논리도 없는 저들은 왜 도청에 들어왔는가. 그녀는 동료들을 전적으로 신뢰한다고 자부했으나, 지식인을 향한 신뢰의 부분만큼 동료들에 대한 신뢰를 저버리고 있었던 것은 아닌가, 그녀는 자신을 깊이 자책한다. 그녀는 지금 관통한다. 그녀는 바로 그들이었다. 거기에 잠깐 지식인이 끼어들었던 것이며 그것은 원칙에서 벗어난 것이었으며 이번 항쟁으로 그녀는 다시 동료들에게 돌아온 것이다. 지식인에 대

speak clearly. The man said,

"Isn't leadership what intellectuals do? When the so-called 'Students Committee to Control the Situation' came to the governor's office building complex, the first thing they did was to form a leadership."

"Well, that's the wrong kind of leadership. I'm saying that the true hardliners should form their own leadership."

"Anyhow, we aren't interested in anything like that."

She tried to talk to other people, but their response was the same. Although they were guarding the building with a sense of justice and righteous indignation, they didn't have the ability to form a strong leadership, partially because they had come to the building not as members of an organization, but as individuals. They didn't try to organize and went back to their own posts. Hyeong-ja went back to the kitchen, but couldn't sleep a wink. Something was wrong. Come to think of it, she hadn't seen a single activist in the building. Before this event, Hyeong-ja had met activists many times with Yun Gang-il. She wasn't fond of the idea of "solidarity between laborers and students," but it

해 배신감을 느꼈던 것 자체가 우스운 일이었다. 그것은 배신이 아니고 그들 자체가 바로 그런 성향이 아닌가. 그녀 자신이 흔들렸을 뿐이다.

형자는 동료들을 하나하나 바라보았다. 꼬부라져 잠들기도 하고, 의자에 앉은 채로 잠들기도 하고, 옷을 맨바닥에 깔고 자기도 했다. 그녀는 옆에서 자고 있는 순분의 뺨을 가만히 쓰다듬었다. 순분이가 놀란 듯 눈을 떴다. 의아한 눈빛이 서서히 사라지면서 미소를 지었다. 뺨에 있는 형자의 손을 꼬옥 잡고 가슴께로 가져갔다. 그리고 다시 눈을 감았다. 형자의 눈이 차츰 젖어왔다.

이튿날(25일) 오후 7시가 되어서야 운동권 청년들이 도청에 나타났다. 형자가 알기로는 열 명도 못 되는 인원이었다. 새로 들어온 운동권 청년들이 강경파로 주도권을 쥐면서 도청은 새로운 항쟁 지도부의 면모를 갖추게 되었다. 온건파인 수습위원장은 사의를 표하고 나가버렸다. 식당에서 지금까지 밥 짓는 일을 해왔던 여학생 이십여 명도 함께 빠져나갔다. 인원이 줄어들면서 밥 짓는 일은 더욱 바빠졌다. 밤늦게 YWCA에 대기 중이던 3개 조의 취사부가 새로 편성되어 도청 안으로 들어왔다. 대부분이 근로자들이었다.

was impossible to completely exclude students from their work in a small community like Gwangju. The Democratic Youth group was controlling the leadership among activists. This group was an offshoot of the several hundred college students who initiated the student movement out of righteous indignation against the dictatorship in 1974, when nobody knew any theory or precedents for activism, or had any knowledge of the social sciences. It was natural for them to become leaders of movements. Towards the late 1970s, distinguished men out of office, JOC members,[8] members of the Research Institute of Modern Culture, comprised of former Democratic Youth group members, night school teachers and students, Songbaek Association members,[9] and laborers were carefully joining forces. At first, Hycong-ja was wary of non-labor activists. However, as she got to know them better, she came to like them. Activists were making connections with each other and gathering forces, not through simple theories, offices, and organizations, but based on deep personal trust in each other's moral strength. Nevertheless, she couldn't completely shake off her instinctive distrust of intellectuals. She felt that she could learn from their theories. In theory, they were

밤 10시에 민중민주항쟁 지도부가 정식으로 발족되었다. 야간 경계조가 바뀌는지 복도가 소란스러웠다. 시민군들이 식당 안을 기웃거렸다. 형자는 라면을 끓여주었다. 순분이도 일어나 형자를 도왔다. 라면을 먹던 시민군 중에서 누가 순분이를 보고 눈을 크게 떴다. 그가 말했다.

"아가씨, 나 모르시겠습니까?"

"누구신지……"

"전번에 자전거 태워줬지 않아요."

"어머!"

순분이가 탄성을 올리며 그에게로 다가갔다.

"그땐 정말 고마웠어요."

"여기서 만나게 되다니…… 아가씨도 담이 크네요."

"담이 커서 그러나요? 할 일을 할 뿐인데요."

"이젠 밥도 맘 놓고 먹게 되었구나." 하면서 남자는 하품을 해댔다. 순분이가 말했다.

"빨리 가서 주무세요. 피곤해 보이는데요."

"정말 졸려 죽겠네요. 이틀이나 못 잤어요. 오늘은 괜찮은 먹물들이 들어온 것 같아 잠을 좀 잘 수 있겠네요. 전번 학생수습위원들은 자꾸만 총을 뺏으려고 해서 정말 화가 치밀었어요. 총이 있어야만 도청을 지킬 수 있잖아요.

subscribers to revolutionary ideas, fighters, and pro-gressives. Terms that they ordinarily used like "armed struggle" and "street fight" certainly became part of Hyeong-ja's vocabulary. The sense of betray-al she felt when Yun Gang-il left surged inside her again. "Does this mean that deep down she trusted intellectuals?" When her thoughts reached that point, she suddenly stood up, and looked at her colleagues who were curled up sleeping. Who are they? Why did they come to this building unarmed with any knowledge, theory, or logic of activism? Although she took pride in her complete trust in her fellow workers, she was wondering if she might not have trusted her fellow workers as much as she had trusted intellectuals. She felt a pang of conscience. She had had an epiphany. She was one of them. Intellectuals temporarily wedged themselves between her and her fellow laborers against her principles, and now in the middle of the current struggle she returned to her fellow workers. Her sense of betrayal was itself ridiculous. It wasn't betrayal. It was just their nature. It was she who was wavering.

Hyeong-ja looked at her fellow workers as they slept curled up or sitting in a chair, or on top of

총 없으면 꼼짝없이 당한다구요."

남자는 개머리판을 다정스럽게 쓰다듬었다. 그리고 묻지도 않은 말을 했다.

"아가씨, 내 이름이나 알아두슈. 김두칠이라고 해요."

"내 이름은 순분이에요."

"순분이. 참 이쁘네요. 시골에서 산나물이나 캐야 될 이름인데 참."

"참이라니, 뭐가 참이라는 거예요?"

"못 볼 것 많이 보았을 테니 안됐다는 생각이 들어서요. 나야 사내 새끼니까 괜찮지만……"

순분이의 눈이 금세 젖어왔다.

"그만들 잡시다."

누군가가 말했다. 김두칠은 총대를 어깨에 메고 거수경례를 하고 나가버렸다.

새벽 다섯 시(26일)에 비상령이 떨어졌다. 도청은 삽시간에 긴장감이 감돌았다. 총을 들고 이리저리 뛰어다니기도 했고 창문 밖으로 총부리를 대고 조준하는 시민군도 있었다. 형자는 상황실로 내려가 보았다. 계엄군이 탱크를 앞세우고 시내로 진입하고 있다는 무전이 접수되었다는 것이다. 형자는 뛰어올라와 식당 안에 있는 동료들에

their clothes laid on the floor. She gently touched the cheek of Sunbun, sleeping next to her. Surprised, Sunbun opened her eyes. Wonder was slowly disappearing from her eyes, and she smiled. Holding Hyeong-ja's hand tightly, she brought it near her heart. Then she closed her eyes again. Hyeong-ja's eyes were getting moist.

The next day, May 25th, some young activists showed up at the governor's office building complex only around 7 P.M. There were fewer than ten. These newly arrived activists were hardliners and they took charge of the situation, forming new leadership for the struggle. The committee chair, a moderate, resigned and left. Around twenty female students who had been working in the kitchen left with him. They had to work harder to prepare meals, as there were fewer people. Late at night, three groups came to join the kitchen workers from among people waiting at the YWCA building. Most were laborers.

The People's Democratic Fight leadership was officially inaugurated at 10 P.M. The corridor was noisy due to the changing of the night guard. Citizen soldiers peeped into the kitchen. Hyeong-ja was cooking ramen noodles. Sunbun got up and helped

게 마음을 침착하게 먹고 준비를 하자고 말했다.

"준비라니, 무슨 준비?"

미숙이의 물음에 영순이가 움츠렸던 어깨를 펴며 말을 받았다.

"싸울 준비지 뭐."

"우리에게도 총을 달라고 해야 돼."

"밥만 하니까 속상해. 총 쏘는 법도 배우고 싶어."

"죽게 될지도 모르겠네."

순분이의 말에 모두들 충격을 받은 것 같았다. 순분이도 얼결에 말이 나와 버렸는지 한 손을 입으로 가져갔다.

계엄군은 한국전력 앞에서 진을 치고 더 이상 진격해 들어오지는 않았다. 재야인사들로 이루어진 수습위원들이 계엄군 탱크 앞 도로 위에 드러누웠다는 소식도 들려왔다. 시민들은 아침 일찍부터 도청 앞으로 모여들었다. 항쟁지도부는 계엄군의 일시 진입으로 뒤숭숭한 분위기였지만 어느 정도 체계를 정비하고 있었다.

형자와 순분이는 「투사회보」를 가지러 YWCA로 가는 도중에 분수대 앞에서 궐기대회를 보았다. 시민들이 연단 위에 올라가 하고 싶은 말을 모두 했다. 그러나 하고 싶은 말이라는 것에는 엄격한 기준이 있었다. 그것은 피로써

Hyeong-ja. A citizen soldier, eating ramen, opened his eyes wide when he saw Sunbun. He asked, "Miss, don't you remember me?"

"I wonder..."

"Didn't I gave you a ride on my bicycle?"

"Dear me!"

Sunbun approached him with an exclamation.

"I really appreciate that ride."

"Wow, I get to meet you here... You're brave."

"Do you think it's because I'm brave? I'm just doing what I should do."

"Now I get to eat as much as I want."

He was busy yawning. Sunbun said, "Go get some sleep. You look tired."

"Really, I'm so sleepy. I couldn't sleep a wink for two days. I guess I can sleep tonight, since some decent intellectuals joined us today. Because the previous student committee members kept on trying to take away our guns, I was really angry. We must have guns to protect the governor's office building complex, you know. Without guns, it's over."

The guy lovingly stroked the butt of his rifle. Then he said something unexpected.

"Hey, Miss, why don't you remember my name? It's Kim Du-chil."

찾은 자유를 더럽히지 않는 기준이었고 적에 대한 분명한
응징의 기준이었고 싸움의 양상은 치열한 무장투쟁의 기
준이었다. 자유란 이런 것이 아니겠는가. 무한히 열려 있
는 가능성 앞에서 하나를 선택하는 것이 아니라 상황에
대한 분명한 당위 말이다. 하나의 상황 앞엔 하나의 결정
만이 있을 뿐이다.

계엄군 진입의 소문 때문인지 시민들 사이에 긴장감이
감돌고 있었다.

"언니, 저 벽보 봐."

순분이가 가리킨 곳에 큰 대자보가 붙어 있었다.

미국 항공모함 부산 앞바다에 정박 중.

우리의 우방인 미국은 민주주의와 인권을 수호하는 나
라입니다. 광주의 민주시민을 보호하기 위하여 지금 부산
에 미국 항공모함이 정박 중에 있습니다. 더 이상 광주는
피를 흘리지 않을 것입니다. 시민들은 동요하지 마시고
도청에 집결합시다.

시민들은 그 대자보를 보고 안심하는 눈치였다. 자유의
여신상을 상표로 하는 나라를 떠올리며 막연한 기대감을

"My name is Sunbun."

"Sunbun—that's a very pretty name. That's a name for someone who should be picking wild greens, *tch.*"

"*Tch?* What do you mean by *tch?*"

"I feel sorry that you had to see so many things a human being shouldn't ever have to see. It's ok for me, 'cuz I'm a guy..."

Sunbun's eyes were immediately filled with tears.

"Let's sleep now," someone said.

Kim Du-chil slung his rifle on his shoulder and left the room after giving a military salute.

At 5 A.M. on the 26th an emergency was declared. The governor's office building complex was instantly filled with tension. People were running around with guns, and some citizen soldiers were aiming their rifles outside the windows. Hyeong-ja went downstairs to the operation room. They said that they had received wireless news that martial law enforcement troops were entering downtown led by tanks. Hyeong-ja ran back upstairs and urged her friends in the kitchen to calmly prepare.

"Prepare? Prepare for what?"

When Misuk asked, Yeong-sun answered, shoving back her shoulders, "Prepare for a fight, isn't it?"

갖고 있었는지도 모른다. 나이 많은 할아버지 한 분이 순분에게 물었다.

"뭐라고 썼지? 눈이 어두워서 안 보이는구먼."

순분은 또박또박 읽어주었다. 읽기를 채 끝마치기도 전에 할아버지는 혀를 끌끌 찼다. 순분이가 물었다.

"왜 그러세요, 할아버지?"

"큰 나라는 믿을 것이 못 돼." 하면서 걸음을 옮기는 할아버지 뒤를 형자와 순분은 쫓아갔다. 할아버지는 가로수 밑에 앉아 담배를 붙여 물었다. 그녀들도 옆에 앉았다. 담배 한 대를 다 태우고 나서 혼잣말처럼 할아버지가 중얼거렸다.

"손자놈이 안 들어와 걱정이 태산 같구먼."

"언제부터요?"

"19일이던가, 벌써 일주일이 지났는데……"

"몇 살인데요?"

"고등학생이지. 장손인데 말야."

할아버지 눈가에 눈물이 어른거렸다. 할아버지가 계속해서 말했다.

"병원이란 병원은 다 찾아보았고 상무관에도 도청에도 죄 가보았지. 원 그럴 수가 있는가. 내 평생 그런 처참한

"Let's ask them to give us guns, too."

"I am sad because we've only been cooking. I want to learn to fire a gun, too."

"We might die."

When Sunbun said this, everyone looked shocked. Sunbun, who must have said it in a moment of confusion, quickly covered her mouth with her hand.

The martial law enforcement troops stationed themselves in front of the Korea Electric Power Corporation building but did not advance any further. People said that the distinguished members of the Committee to Control the Situation lay on the road in front of the tanks. Citizens gathered in front of the governor's office building complex from early morning on. The leadership had been a little distracted by the advance of the martial law enforcement troops, but calm and order had been somewhat restored.

Hyeong-ja and Sunbun went to the YWCA building to get the *Fighter's Newsletter*, and on their way they saw a rally at the plaza in front of the fountain. People went up to the platform and said whatever they wanted to say. But their words conformed to certain strict standards. All tried not to sully the freedom they had acquired through bloodshed, all

모습은 처음 보았지. 짐승도 그러지는 못하는 법이여, 짐 승도. 하늘도 무심하시지."

할아버지는 하늘을 쳐다보며 깊은 한숨을 내쉬었다. 하늘은 맑고 푸르렀다. 무심한 하늘은 그 빛을 찬란히 드러내고 있었다. 군용기가 요란한 소리를 내며 날아갔다. 분수대 연단 위에서는 웬 아낙네가 눈물 어린 목소리로 외치고 있었다. 형자가 할아버지에게로 눈을 돌리며 물었다.

"할아버지, 아까 하신 말씀인데요. 큰 나라는 믿을 것이 못 된다고 하셨잖아요."

"그게 뭐 어때서?"

"왜 그런 말씀을 하셨나 하고 여쭈어보는 거예요."

"늙은이가 뭐 아나? 경험으로 미루어봐서 무심코 나온 거지."

"경험이라니요? 어떤 경험요?"

할아버지는 대답을 않고 담배만 뻐끔뻐끔 피웠다. 담배 연기를 바라보는 할아버지의 시선이 가늘어졌다. 할아버지는 말하기 시작했다.

6·25사변 때 할아버지는 국방군에 입대해서 평양까지 밀고 올라갔다. 코 큰 병사들까지 합세해서 파죽지세로

clearly wanted to punish their enemy, and all were in favor of fierce armed struggle. Wouldn't this be a model for true freedom? Not to choose one among infinite possibilities, but to choose what the situation calls for? There should be only one choice for each situation.

Probably because of rumors about the advance of the martial law enforcement troops, the atmosphere at the rally was tense.

"Eonni, look at that poster!" Sunbun pointed.

"American Aircraft Carrier Mooring at Sea off Busan:

America, our ally, defends democracy and human rights. An American aircraft carrier is currently mooring at sea off Busan in order to protect the citizens of Gwangju. Gwangju won't bleed any more. Citizens, let's not be worried and gather in front of the governor's office building complex."

People looked relieved after reading this message. Probably the Statue of Liberty they pictured in their minds, symbol of America, encouraged a vague expectation. An elderly man asked Sunbun, "What does that say? I can't read because of my eyesight."

밀고 올라갈 땐 신나기까지 했다. 그들이 평양에 입성했을 땐 이미 쑥밭이 돼 있었다. 시가는 말할 것도 없고 교외 부근까지 하나도 남아 있는 것이 없었다. 유엔군의 무차별 폭격 때문이었다. 살아 있는 것은 모조리 요리해버려 그야말로 죽음의 도시였다.

"······은근히 부아가 치밀더군."

할아버지의 음성에 노기가 띠어 있었다.

"왜요?"

"아, 왜 평양이라고 하면 우리나라 도시 중에서 경치 좋기로 유명하잖아. 나도 소학교 때 수학여행 가봐서 알지. 아무리 빨갱이들이 판치고 있던 도시라도 역시 우리나라가 아닌가. 그런 도시를 코 큰 놈들이 와서 쑥밭을 만들어 놓았으니 화가 안 나고 배기겠어? 이겼다는 생각보다 금수강산이 초토화됐다는 생각이 앞서더구만. 그때 큰 나라는 믿을 수 없다는 생각이 들었지. 믿을 건 제 민족밖에 더 있겠어? 싸우네 마네 해도 제 새끼, 제 가족, 제 동족이 제일 중요하지 않겠나. 살붙이니까. 딴 나라는 믿을 것이 못 된다니까······"

말을 마친 할아버지는 타버린 담뱃재를 털어냈다.

이렇게 오래 살았다는 것은 그 나름만큼 지혜롭게 되는

Sunbun read it out loud. Even before she finished reading, he clucked his tongue. Sunbun asked, "What's the matter, Grandpa?"

"One shouldn't trust a big country."

After saying this, the elderly man walked away. Hyeong-ja and Sunbun followed him. He sat down under a roadside tree and lit a cigarette. The girls sat next to him. After finishing the cigarette, he muttered, as if to himself, "I am extremely worried. My grandson didn't come home."

"Since when?"

"The nineteenth, I believe. It's already been a week..."

"How old is he?"

"He's a high school student. He's my eldest grandson by my eldest son."

The elderly man was tearing up. He continued, "I've been to all the hospitals, and the Sangmu Building as well as the governor's office building complex. How could this be? I have never seen such cruel sights. Even animals wouldn't do that, even animals... Heaven help us!"

Looking up at the sky, he sighed heavily. The sky was clear, an unconcerned and brilliant blue. A military plane flew over with a loud roar. On the plat-

것인가, 하고 형자는 생각해보았다. 아니면 이 민족이 노인들을 지혜롭게 만드는 것인가. 자애롭고 평안한 노후가 아니라 민족이 겪어온 수난들을 되살리며 회한에 젖기도 하고, 분노가 불끈 솟아오르기도 하고, 때로는 무력감에 빠져 하루하루 사는 것 이외에는 어떠한 생존의 기쁨도 없고, 때때로 현 정세를 본능적으로 감지할 수 있는 지혜를 체득하기도 한다.

살아 있는 자들은 정치적이다. 아무리 혼자 무력감에 빠져 있어도 계기가 주어지면 정치성의 면모가 드러난다. 반골이든 반동이든 야당세든 여당세든…… 정치적 입장을 갖는다는 것은 참으로 중요하다. 올바른 정치적 입장은 삶의 방향을 올바르게 결정짓는다. 광주는 지금 정치적 입장을 분명히 하고 있다. 군사 독재 정권은 물러가야 한다. 군사 독재 정권이 만들어낸 공공건물이 불타 버린 것을 보면 안다. 싸움의 격렬함치고는 건물은 그리 많이 파괴되지 않았다. 꼭 없애야 될 곳만 불태워 없앴다. MBC, 세무서, 노동청, 어용 언론, 어용 노조, 민중의 기본권이 박탈된 곳만 정확하게 파괴되었다. 이 사실은 이 항쟁이 절대로 무정부주의자들이나 폭도들의 싸움이 아니라는 점을 드러내준다. 도청을 불태워 버릴 수도 있었다.

form in front of the fountain, a woman was shouting with a trembling voice. Turning towards the elderly man, Hyeong-ja asked, "Grandpa, about what you said earlier... You said that one shouldn't trust a big country, right?"

"Yes. So?"

"I'm just wondering why you think that."

"What would an old man know? I said that without thinking, just from my experience."

"Experience? What's your experience?"

Without answering, he continued to puff on his cigarette. Gazing at the cigarette smoke, his eyes grew distant. He began talking.

During the Korean War, he volunteered for the National Defense Forces and went up to Pyeong-yang. It was even exciting when they were advancing with overwhelming power together with big-nose troops.[10] When they entered Pyeong-yang, it was a wasteland. Nothing remained even in the suburbs, let alone downtown. It was because of the indiscriminate bombing. All things living had been wiped out, and Pyeong-yang was literally a city of death.

"...I got angry in my heart."

There was anger in his voice.

그러나 도청은 건재하다. 그것은 우리들이 정치를 하겠다는 의지이다. 진정한 민주 정부를 수립하겠다는 표현이다. 정치의 현실성을 획득하겠다는 행동이다.

할아버지가 자리를 털고 일어섰다. 순분이가 부축하며 말했다.

"가시게요?"

"손자놈 친구들이라도 찾아봐야 하겠구먼. 혹 소식이라도 들을 수 있을는지."

굽은 등을 취적취적 흔들며 걸어가는 할아버지를 그녀들은 한동안 바라보았다. 그녀들은 똑같이 손자는 죽었을 거라는 생각을 했다.

궐기대회 연단 위에서는 웬 스님이 목청을 돋우고 있었다. 장삼 자락이 바람에 휘날려 장중한 분위기를 자아내고 있었다. ×××목을 쳐서 이 장삼 자락으로 싸갖고 오겠다는 대목에서 군중은 열광하면서 박수를 쳤다. 순분이도 박수를 치다가 골똘한 표정이 되어 있는 형자를 보고 조심스럽게 물었다.

"언니, 그래도 미국은 좋은 나라잖아. 어쨌든 우리를 도우러 온다니까."

"글쎄, 난 할아버지 말씀이 맞을 것 같아. 우린 군사 독

"Why?"

"Well, Pyeong-yang is known among our cities for its beautiful scenery, right? I know because I went there on a field trip during elementary school. It belongs to our country no matter how riddled it was with Reds. How could I not be angry when big-nose guys came and turned such a city to ruins? I couldn't help thinking about the devastation of our beautiful land even before celebrating our victory. It was then that I realized we shouldn't trust big countries. Wouldn't our people be the only trustworthy ones? Even if we fight with each other, wouldn't it be our children, our family, and our people that are most important? Because we're related. Other countries can't be trusted..."

The elderly man shook the ashes from his cigarette.

Hyeong-ja wondered: does living long mean becoming wiser like this? Or maybe it's this nation that makes old men wiser? Most of them cannot enjoy a loving and peaceful old age. Instead, they end up recalling—sometimes poignantly and other times angrily—all the suffering they have undergone, living in depression without feeling any joy, and occasionally gaining insight into the current

재 정권에 의해 피를 흘렸거든. 그리고 미국은 군사 독재 정권을 인정하고 옹호하지."

"……"

"생각해봐, 순분아. 우리 국군의 군사작전권을 누가 갖고 있는 줄 아니?"

순분은 고개를 가로저었다. 형자가 말을 이었다.

"서울만 빼놓고 한미연합사령관이 갖고 있어. 그리고 연합사령관은 미국인이야."

"그러는 게 어됐대?"

"그렇다니까. 너 텔레비에서 가끔 판문점 회담 장면을 보여주는 거 봤지? 이북은 분명 이북 대표자가 나오는데 이남은 미국인 대표자로 나가잖아. 남의 나라에 와서 주인 행세를 하는 격이지."

순분이의 입술에 파르르 경련이 일어났다. 막연했던 부분들이 환하게 명확해지면서 순분은 기쁨과 분노의 감정을 동시에 맛보았다. 형자가 말했다.

"분명한 건, 광주가 또다시 계엄군에 함락되려면 미국의 동의가 있어야만 되는 거야."

"그렇겠지."

"우린 미국에 대해서 막연한 환상을 갖고 있어. 어쩌면

state of affairs thanks to the wisdom they acquired over the years that became second nature to them.

People who are alive are political. No matter how alone and helpless they may be, they become political when called upon, whether they are defiant or reactionary, or in favor of the ruling party or the opposition party... It is very important to take a political stance. A righteous political position guides one to a righteous life. Gwangju is now taking a clear political stance. The military dictatorship should be driven out. That's what the burning down of public buildings built by the military dictatorship means. Despite the violent nature of the fight, only a few buildings—only those that needed to be done away with—were destroyed: MBC, the Revenue Office, Labor Office, Kept Press, and Company Unions. They were the prime agents in depriving the grassroots of basic human rights. That meant this fight wasn't a fight of anarchists or mobsters. They could have burned down the governor's office building complex, but the building was left standing. That represented their will to self-govern, i.e. a will to establish a true democratic government. It meant that they wanted to acquire real political power.

미국의 정체를 분명하게 깨닫게 해주는 일일 거야."

"뭐가?"

"만의 하나라도 도청이 함락되고 우리가 저들의 총에 맞아 죽게 된다면, 그땐 미국의 정체를 분명히 깨닫게 될 거야."

"……"

"져도 지는 것이 아닐 수 있어. 그래도 이런 엄청난 피의 대가로 알게 되는 것이 슬퍼."

형자의 목소리가 떨려 나왔다. 순분이가 형자의 손을 잡으며 조금 흔들었다.

"언니, 자꾸만 지는 쪽으로만 생각하는 것 같아."

"그렇구나. 내가 왜 이러지. 이러면 안 되지. 우린 승리할 수 있어."

하면서 순분의 손을 같이 흔들었다. 승리를 하려면 구체적인 전략이 세워져야 한다. 형자의 머릿속에 여러 작전들이 떠올랐다.

미국인들을 인질로 잡아 도청 안에 가둔다. 계엄군이 진압해 오면 같이 자폭한다고 위협한다. 자국민 인명은 하늘같이 존중하는 미국 정부에서 모종의 협의를 제기한다. 최소치는 인명 피해가 더 이상 없을 것이고, 최대치는

The elderly man stood up, brushing off the dirt.

"Are you leaving?"

"I'd like to look for my grandson's friends. Who knows, they might know where he is."

They watched him walking away, his bent back swaying sideways. They all thought simultaneously that his grandson must have been killed.

On the platform at the rally, a Buddhist monk was loudly making a speech. The hem of his broad-sleeved robe was fluttering in the wind, and the atmosphere was solemn. When he said that he would cut XXX's head off, wrap it in his robe, and bring it back, the crowd started enthusiastically cheering and clapping. Sunbun also clapped, and carefully asked Hyeong-ja, who seemed to be absorbed in her thoughts, a question:

"Eonni, isn't America still a good country? At any rate, they are coming to help us."

"Well, I think that grandpa is right. Our blood was shed at the hands of the military dictatorship. Yet, America acknowledges that regime and defends it, too."

"......"

"Think about it, Sunbun. Do you know who commands the Korean military?"

이 도시만이라도 해방구로 고수하며 지방자치제를 실시한다. 또 다른 작전도 떠올랐다. 특공대를 조직한다. 무기를 갖고 도시를 빠져나간다. 타 도시의 미국 대사관을 점거한다. 그러면 계엄군의 진격을 막을 수 있고 시간을 벌면서 해방구의 정치적 진로를 펴나간다.

항쟁지도부 저녁 회의 때 이 작전들을 꼭 제시해야겠다고 형자는 마음먹었다. 항쟁지도부가 새로 발족된 것은 어제였고 체계가 잡혀가면 이러한 작전들이 수행될 것은 자명한 일이었다.

군중들은 선창자를 따라 구호를 외치고 있었다.

그녀들은 YWCA로 갔다. 그곳은 선동선전대인 '광대' 문화팀들과 「투사회보」팀인 야학생들의 거점이었다. 영철이는 잠을 거의 못 잤는지 핏발이 선 눈을 하고 있었다. 「투사회보」팀을 이끌어가고 있는 용준이는 속속 들어오는 속보들을 검토하며 편집을 하고 있었다. 조직되어 있던 두 팀은 최대한 능력을 발휘하고 있었다. 조직은 이렇게 중요하다. 조직은 일상 속에서 이루어지며 일상 속에서의 싸움이다. 조직의 일원으로서 작은 일이라도 겸허하고 꾸준하게 하는 것은 더 본격적인 조직을 준비하고 예고하는 일이기도 하다. 조직은 현실이다. 그러한 현실은 사상을

Sunbun shook her head sideways. Hyeong-ja continued, "Except for Seoul, the commander-in-chief of the ROK-U.S. Combined Forces Command commands it. The commander-in-chief is American."

"How could that be?"

"That's how it is. You've seen the talks in Panmunjom on TV from time to time, right? North Korea sends their delegates, but South Korea sends Americans as our delegates. Americans play the host in a foreign country."

Sunbun's lips trembled. Things that had been vague suddenly became clear, and Sunbun felt joy and anger at the same time. Hyeong-ja said, "What's clear is that Gwangju can fall to the martial law enforcement troops only under the auspices of America."

"I guess so."

"We all have vague illusions about America. Perhaps this incident will help us understand America more clearly."

"What?"

"If in the worst case scenario the governor's office building complex falls and we perish at their hands, then our people will know the true nature of America."

향해 고양되어나간다. 조직은 물리력이다. 지금 이 두 조직은 몇십 만의 시민을 결집시키고, 홍보를 담당하고, 사건의 진상을 규명한다. 조직의 물리력을 눈으로 확인하면서 형자는 감격에 겨워 눈시울이 뜨거워졌다.

누군가 용준이를 불러냈다. 잠시 후에 들어온 용준이의 표정이 굳어 있었다. 영철이가 물었다.

"왜 그래, 형?"

"오늘 밤 중으로 계엄군이 진격해 올 가능성이 많다는 연락을 받았어."

비장한 침묵이 흘렀다. 드디어 올 것이 오는 모양이구나. 사람들은 서로의 얼굴을 보지 않고 각자의 생각에 깊이 잠기는 듯했다. 눈에 눈물이 고이는 사람도 있었다. 또다시 처절한 죽음의 항쟁을 하여야 할 것인가. 죽어간 영령들 곁으로 가야 할 것인가. 누군가가 노래를 부르기 시작했다.

우리의 소원은 통일

꿈에도 소원은 통일

이 정성 다해서 통일

통일을 이루자

"……"

"Sometimes, losing isn't really losing. Still, I'm sad that we've gained this knowledge as a result of such enormous bloodshed."

Hyeong-ja's voice was trembling. Sunbun took her hand and gently shook her.

"Eonni, you seem to think that we'll lose."

"You're right. Why am I doing that? I shouldn't. We can win." Saying this, she grasped Sunbun's hand. To win, one should have a concrete strategy. Hyeong-ja began to think of various strategies.

'We could take Americans hostage in the governor's office building complex. When the martial law enforcement troops come, we threaten to blow up the building. Since Americans respect the lives of their own people above all, the American government will try to negotiate. At least there won't be any more bloodshed, and if things go well, it's possible that we can keep this city as a liberated area and establish a local self-government.' Then she thought of another strategy. 'We organize a commando unit. The unit will sneak out of the city and occupy an American Embassy building in another city. Then we can stop the advance of the martial law enforcement troops and buy time to plan a

"그래도 일은 해야지."

용준은 소매를 걷어붙이고 등사기 쪽으로 다가갔다.

형자와 순분은 그곳을 나왔다. 날이 어두워지고 있었다. 고립된 도시는 외로운 싸움 끝에 허물어져 가고 있었다. 궐기대회는 끝났지만 시민들은 흩어지지 않고 「우리의 소원」을 부르고 있었다.

이 겨레 살리는 통일
이 나라 살리는 통일
통일이여 어서 오라
통일이여 오라

아무도 움직이려고 하지 않았다. 이런 상태에서 계엄군과 싸워 시민군이 이길 것이라고 생각하는 시민은 거의 없었다. 식량의 공급도 막혀 있었고 슬픔과 피해 의식이 고개를 쳐들기 시작했다. 군중들은 고개를 숙이고 흩어지기 시작했다. 순분이가 젖은 눈으로 형자를 바라보며 말했다.

"언니, 아무래도 계엄군이 쳐들어오려나 봐."

형자가 고개를 끄덕였다.

political way to secure the liberated area.'

Hyeong-ja decided to discuss these proposals during the evening meeting. The leadership had been formed only yesterday. Once they settled down, they could definitely carry out these strategies.

Crowds were shouting slogans, following a leader.

They went to the YWCA building. There was the "Gwangdae (clown)" Culture Team, in charge of propaganda, as well as the *Fighter's Newsletter* Team, made up of night school students. Yeong-cheol's eyes were bloodshot, probably because he hadn't slept in days. Yong-jun, the editor-in-chief of the *Fighter's Newsletter*, was examining up-to-the-minute news and editing the newspaper. The two teams, which had been well organized before this event, were working with exceptional efficiency. 'Organization is important. We form an organization in our everyday lives. An organization is formed through our everyday struggles. A member of an organization who modestly and persistently works on even a small task is also preparing for, and anticipating, the building of a fuller organization. An organization is a concrete thing. This concrete thing develops into its ideal form. An organization has concrete power. Now these two groups, the two

"순분아."

형자의 목소리가 낮게 가라앉아 있어 순분은 긴장했다. 그녀들은 도청과 분수대 사이에 서 있었다. 길게 뻗어 나간 금남로에 하나 둘씩 불빛이 빛나기 시작했고, 어디서 날아왔는지 새 떼들이 분수대 위를 빙빙 돌았다. 형자는 마치 처음 보는 풍경인 양 하나하나 시선을 주었다. 순분이가 참지 못하고 그녀의 팔을 잡았다.

"언니, 뭘 생각해?"

"음……"

낮게 신음 소리를 내며 형자는 말을 이었다.

"분수대 앞과 YWCA, 그리고 도청."

"……"

"순분아 생각해봐. 그곳에 모인 사람들의 선택을."

"……"

"분수대 앞에 모인 사람들은 일상으로 돌아가는 사람들이야. YWCA는 언제든지 선택의 가능성이 있는 사람들이 모인 곳이고, 그리고 도청은……"

"도청은?"

순분이가 다급하게 물었다. 형자가 도청으로 시선을 돌리며 말했다.

organizations, unite a few hundred thousand citizens, take charge of propaganda, and establish truths.' Realizing the concrete power of an organization, Hyeong-ja was moved to tears.

Someone called Yong-jun out of the room. He returned a little later with a stern expression. Yeong-cheol asked, "What's the matter, Hyeong?"

"I heard that the martial law enforcement troops will probably advance tonight."

The room fell silent. It was a tragic and brave silence. 'Finally, what has been anticipated is coming.' People, perhaps deep in thought, didn't look at each other. Some were tearing up. 'Do we have to fight a bloody battle again? Shall we join the spirits of the fallen heroes?' Someone began singing.

Our wish is unification.
Even in our dreams, it is unification.
With all our hearts, it is unification.
Let's bring about unification.

"We still have work to do."
Yong-jun rolled up his sleeves and headed towards a mimeograph machine.
Hyeong-ja and Sunbun left the building. It was

"도청은 죽음을 결단하는 사람들의 것이야. 그것은 선택이 아니라 당위로 받아들이는 사람들의 것이지."

형자가 마치 자신에게 확신시키려는 듯이 두 손을 모아잡았다. 순분은 그 손 위에 자신의 손도 포개었다.

"내 말을 잘 들어봐. 나중에 누군가가 이 일을 해야 돼. 어쩜 너희들이 해야 될지도 몰라."

형자가 말했다. 순분은 잡고 있던 손에 힘을 주었다. 형자가 말을 이었다.

"도청에 끝까지 남아 있던 사람들을 잘 기억해둬. 어떤 사람들이 이 항쟁에 가담했고 투쟁했고 죽었는가를 꼭 기억해야 돼."

"……"

"그러면 너희들은 알게 될 거야. 어떤 사람들이 역사를 만들어가는가를…… 그것은 곧 너희들의 힘이 될 거야."

형자의 눈이 먼 곳을 응시하고 있었다. 깊이를 알 수 없는 눈빛이 있다. 머리카락이 바람에 나부꼈다. 이마에 흩어진 머리카락을 순분이가 조심스럽게 쓸어주었다. 언니는 꼭 죽으려고 마음먹은 것 같아, 하고 말하고 싶었으나 속으로 삼켰다. 순분이가 말했다.

"언니, 난 그래. 이 며칠간 맛본 해방의 기쁨만으로도

getting dark. The isolated city was falling after a lonely fight. Although the rally was over, people were singing the song "Our Wish."

Unification will revive our people.
Unification will revive our country.
Come, hurry, you unification!
Come, unification!

Nobody moved. Nobody in the citizen's army was thinking they could really win against the martial law enforcement troops. Their food supply was cut off. They began to feel a sense of sadness and loss. Crowds with their heads hung low began dispersing. Looking at Hyeong-ja with tear-filled eyes, Sunbun said,

"Eonni, I guess the martial law enforcement troops are marching in."

Hyeong-ja nodded and said, "Sunbun!"

Hyeong-ja's voice was low, and Sunbun braced herself. They were standing between the fountain and the governor's office building complex. Streetlights began coming on one by one along Geumnam-ro Street. A flock of birds flew in from somewhere and was circling above the fountain.

일생 동안 어떤 험난한 일을 당하더라도 참아낼 수 있을
것 같아."

"그럼, 그렇구말구."

그녀들은 도청 안으로 들어갔다.

작전상황실에 시민군들이 부산스럽게 드나들고 있었
다. 무전을 듣고 있는 상황실장의 표정이 어두웠다. 기동
타격대장이 급한 걸음으로 상황실로 들어갔다. 형자는 순
분에게 먼저 취사실로 가라고 이르고 기동타격대원 중의
한 사람을 붙들고 물어보았다.

"총 한 자루만 얻을 수 있을까요?"

"왜요?"

"아무래도 필요할 것 같아서요."

"총은 있지만 총알이 형편없이 모자라요."

기동타격대원은 바쁜 듯이 가버렸다. 형자는 각 분대실
을 기웃거려보다가 총알이 없는 M1 한 자루를 습득하게
되었다. 워낙 고물이 되어 폐기 처분이 된 것 같았다. 손
잡이 부분이 너덜너덜하고 개머리판과 총신의 결합이 불
량하여 몹시 흔들거렸다. 그래도 안도감으로 마음이 진정
되어왔다. 두 손으로 부여안았다. 뺨에 총신을 갖다댔다.
섬뜩했다. 그러나 뺨의 온기가 총신에 전해지면서 마치

Hyeong-ja stared at each thing around her one by one, as if looking at them for the first time. Unable to stand it any longer, Sunbun grabbed her by the arm.

"Eonni, what are you thinking?"

"Mmm..."

Moaning in a low voice, Hyeong-ja continued.

"The square in front of the fountain, the YWCA building, and the governor's office building complex."

"......"

"Think about the choices made by people gathering in those places."

"......"

"People who gather at the plaza in front of the fountain are people who always go back to their daily lives. Those who gather at the YWCA building can always choose to go back. And those in the governor's office building complex..."

"Yes?" Sunbun asked quickly. Turning her eyes towards the governor's office, Hyeong-ja said, "The governor's office building complex is the place for those willing to risk their lives. A place for those who consider risking their lives not as a matter of choice but as what one ought to do."

늘 대해 오던 일상의 물건처럼 다정스러웠다.

기동타격대장이 상황실에서 나왔다. 기동타격대원들이 대오를 정비하고 급히 도청을 떠나갔다. 외곽 지대를 방어하기 위해서였다. 2개조는 도청 사수를 위해 남았다.

형자는 취사실로 갔다. 총을 든 형자를 보고 모두들 놀라는 것 같았다. 그녀가 말했다.

"형편없이 망가져서 내버려진 것을 가져온 것뿐이야."

저녁은 먹는 둥 마는 둥했다. 취사실을 기웃거리는 시민군이 거의 없었다. 그녀들은 식사를 하라고 각 분대실을 찾아가보았다. 모두들 정신이 없는지 들은 척 하지 않았다. 할 수 없이 쟁반에 식사를 받쳐 들고 분대실로 찾아가 억지로라도 밥을 먹였다. 지금 밥 먹게 생겼냐고 핀잔을 주기도 했지만 억지로 입 속에 넣으면서 눈물이 핑 돌기도 했다.

작전상황실은 숨 가쁘게 돌아가고 있었다. 무전을 듣고 있던 상황실장은 순분이가 내미는 쟁반을 손으로 가볍게 밀치면서 나가라고 손짓했다. 상황실장이 숨 가쁘게 소리쳤다.

"여기는 도청본부다."

"뭐라고?"

As if trying to convince herself, Hyeong-ja clasped her hands together. Sunbun held them in hers.

"Listen to me carefully. Somebody will have to do this later. Perhaps it is you who will do it," said Hyeong-ja.

Sunbun clutched her hands tightly. Hyeong-ja continued, "Do remember those who stayed in the governor's office building complex to the last. You must remember those who took part in this struggle and died."

"......"

"Then, you'll know who makes history. That knowledge will make you stronger."

Hyeong-ja was looking far away. The light in her eyes was unfathomable. Her hair was fluttering in the wind. Sunbun carefully combed Hyeong-ja's hair over her forehead with her fingers. Although she felt like saying, 'You sound like you've decided to die,' she swallowed her words. Instead, she said, "Eonni, as for me, thanks to this happiness that I tasted after liberation during the last few days, I feel as if I can get through whatever tough situation comes my way during the rest of my life."

"I have no doubt."

They entered the governor's office building com-

"잘 안 들린다. 크게 말하라, 오버."

"뭐라고? 화정동 시민군 본부라고?"

"응 응."

"뭐? 수십 대의 탱크로 밀어붙여 쳐들어온다고?"

"응 응. 지원군을 보내달라고?"

"지원군이 어딨어. 도청 사수 인원도 부족한데."

"총알도 부족해? 여기도 마찬가지야."

상황실장의 얼굴에 진땀이 흘렀다.

취사부에 한 청년이 들어왔다. 그가 말했다.

"지금 계엄군이 진격해 들어오고 있습니다. 나이 어린 학생이나 여자들은 피신하라는 지도부의 명령입니다."

"오빠들과 같이 있겠어요."

영순이가 말했다.

"우리에게도 총을 주세요."

"우리도 싸우겠어요."

이곳저곳에서 울음이 터져 나왔다. 한 여자애는 청년이 메고 있는 총을 달라고까지 했다. 청년은 가슴이 미어지는지 꿀꺽하고 침을 삼켰다. 그는 목소리를 가다듬고 명령조로 말했다.

"빨리 나가십시오. 시간이 없습니다. 이건 명령입니다.

plex.

The citizen's army troops were busily coming in and going out of the Operation Room. The operation chief was listening to the radio with a gloomy face. The Special Strike Force captain rushed into the room. After sending Sunbun to the kitchen, Hyeong-ja asked a member of the Special Strike Force, "May I get a gun?"

"Why?"

"I think it's about time for me to have one."

"We have guns, but we're short of bullets."

The Special Strike Force member rushed out. After looking around various rooms, Hyeong-ja found a gun without ammunition. It seemed that this gun was available only because it was so old that it had been discarded. The handle was scruffy and the butt plate and gun barrel were so loosely connected that they were rattling. Still, Hyeong-ja felt relieved and secure. Holding the gun in her arms, she brought the barrel to her cheek. It was startlingly cold. But when it was warmed by her cheek, it started to feel pleasant, like an everyday object.

The chief of the Special Strike Force came out of the Operation Room. Members of the Special Strike Force hurriedly emerged from the building complex

살아서 중언할 사람도 있어야 하잖습니까?"

모두들 흐느꼈다. 청년은 말을 잇지 못하고 나가버렸다. 나가지 않겠다고 버티는 동료들을 하나하나 내보내면서 형자는 결코 눈물을 보이지 않았다. 나가는 동료들 중에 순분이가 마지막으로 문을 나서면서 흐느꼈다.

"언니."

"그래, 잘 가."

순분은 복도를 걸어나가다가 김두칠을 만났다. 그는 엉겁결에 순분의 손을 꽉 쥐었다. 순분의 눈물이 김두칠의 손등에 떨어졌다. 김두칠은 손을 놓고 그녀의 등을 밀었다. 차마 걸음을 떼어 놓을 수 없는지 벽에 손을 의지하며 걸음을 떼어 놓았다. 막 계단을 내려서면서 그녀가 무어라고 소리쳤으나 사람들의 술렁거림 속에 그냥 파묻혀 버렸다. 김두칠은 흐르는 눈물을 얼른 손등으로 씻었다. 그리고 도청 광장으로 나 있는 창문 앞으로 다가섰다. 그를 따라온 두 명의 시민군도 같이 나란히 섰다. 식당 문에 기대어 있던 형자도 그들 곁으로 다가갔다.

창문으로 5월의 바람이 불어오고 있었다. 시가지는 깊은 정적에 싸여 있었다. 하늘과 땅이 검은 장막을 하나로 휘두른 것같이 분간이 없었다. 별똥별 하나가 포물선을

in formation. They were going to defend the city from its outskirts. Two teams remained to defend the building to the death.

Hyeong-ja went to the kitchen. Seeing her holding a gun, everyone seemed surprised. Hyeong-ja said, "I just picked up a gun that was abandoned because it was totally broken."

People weren't that interested in dinner. The citizen's army soldiers rarely came to the kitchen, so the women went around to different rooms to invite people to dinner. Absorbed in what they were doing, nobody paid attention. As a last resort, the women brought food in on a tray, insisting that the soldiers eat. Some balked, saying it wasn't a time to eat, but others, with tears in their eyes, were forcing food into their mouths.

Things were happening at a frantic pace in the Operation Room. Listening to the radio, the Operation Room chief gently pushed back the tray Sunbun offered, motioning her to leave. He shouted breathlessly into the radio.

"The governor's office building complex."

"What?"

"I cannot hear very well. Speak loudly, over!"

"What? The Hwajeong-dong headquarters of the

그리며 사라졌다. 바람이 세차게 불어왔다. 그들은 가로수가 서걱이는 것 같은 소리를 들었다. 풀 향기 같은 냄새도 맡은 것 같았다. 김두칠은 숨을 크게 들이마셨다. 그가 혼잣말처럼 중얼거렸다.

"이렇게 좋은 세상인데……"

옆에 서 있는 시민군이 고개를 끄덕였다. 뺨 한쪽에 상처 자국이 나 있었지만 표정은 맑고 진지했다. 또 한 시민군은 열다섯, 여섯쯤이나 되어 보이는 소년이었다. 총을 어깨에 멘 것이 힘겨운 듯 한쪽 어깨가 처져 있었다. 소년이 말했다.

"이상하게 식구들이 둘러앉아 밥 먹던 것이 생각나요."

소년이 잠시 말을 끊었다가 다시 이었다.

"그때는 밥을 먹어도 먹어도 밥숟갈만 내려놓고 뒤돌아서면 다시 배가 고팠는데 여기서는 하루에 겨우 한 끼 정도밖에 먹지 못하는데도 배고픈 줄 모르겠어요. 그냥 모든 게 안심이 되고 좋아요."

소년은 자랑스러운 듯 총대를 슬그머니 만졌다. 그리고 형자를 바라보며 물었다.

"누나도 총 있어요?"

"그래, 있어."

citizen's army?"

"Yes, yes."

"What? Dozens of tanks pressing into the city?"

"Yes, yes. You need more backup forces?"

"What backup forces? We don't have enough people to defend our building."

"You're short of bullets? We don't have them,
either."

The chief of the Operation Room was sweating.

A young man entered the kitchen. He said, "The
martial law enforcement troops are advancing now.
The leaders have ordered that young students and
women to get out of the building."

"We'll remain with you, brothers," said Yeong-sun.

"Please give us guns."

"We'll fight, too."

Women were bursting into tears here and there. A
girl asked the young man to please give her his
rifle. Moved and heartbroken, the young man swallowed hard. Controlling his voice, he ordered stern-
ly, "Please hurry up and leave. We don't have time.
This is an order. We need survivors who will testify,
too, don't we?"

Everyone was sobbing. Unable to speak another
word, the young man left. Forcing her friends, who

"그럼 됐네요."

먼 곳에서 연발총 소리가 났다. 우리 편 총성이 아니다. 형자는 총성만 들어도 우리 편인지 아닌지 구별할 수 있다. 우리 편은 둔탁하고 탁, 탁, 탁, 끊어지는 소리가 난다. 김두칠이 윗주머니에서 담배 한 개비를 꺼냈다.

"담배가 있었군."

뺨에 상처 자국이 나 있는 시민군이 반가운 듯 말했다.

"겨우 한 대 얻었지요."

성냥불을 그었다. 잠시 밝아졌다. 불만 붙이고 담배를 건네주었다.

"형 먼저 피세요."

"자네 먼저 피워."

"먼저 피세요."

그들은 한 모금씩 번갈아 피웠다. 중간쯤 태웠을 때 김두칠이 소년에게 담배를 내밀었다.

"너도 한 모금 피워라."

"전 담배 피울 줄 몰라요."

"그래도 피워, 임마. 어쩌면 마지막 담배가 될지도 모르니까……"

소년은 두 손으로 받아들고 조심히 한 모금 빨았다. 평

insisted on remaining, to leave one by one, Hyeong-ja didn't shed a single tear. Leaving last, Sunbun sobbed.

"Eonni," she called Hyeong-ja.

"Yes, dear. Good-bye."

Sunbun ran into Kim Du-chil in the corridor. He held her hands tightly in a moment of confusion. Sunbun's tears fell on the backs of his hands. Letting her go, he gently pushed her. He seemed to be having a hard time walking. He was slowly moving forward, touching the wall. As Sunbun headed downstairs, she shouted something to him, but her voice was drowned out in the commotion. Kim Du-chil quickly wiped the tears from his face with the back of his hand. He then went to a window facing the plaza in front of the building. Two Citizens' Army soldiers followed and stood next to him. Hyeong-ja, who had been leaning on the door of the dining hall, also approached.

The May breeze was blowing in through the window. The city was enveloped in a deep silence. They couldn't tell sky from earth, as if they were behind a black curtain. A shooting star drew a parabola before disappearing into the night. The wind became gustier. They could hear something

소에 담배 연기라면 몹시도 싫어하던 형자였지만 오늘따라 그 냄새가 살냄새처럼 향기롭게 느껴졌다.

"누나도 한 모금 피세요."

"난 이미 피운 것 같은 느낌이야."

형자는 문득 이들이 오래 전에 잃었던 형제들이 아닌가 하는 느낌이 들었다. 눈물이 솟구쳐 오를 것 같아 눈을 몇 번 깜빡거렸다. 김두칠이 그녀의 어깨를 서너 번 토닥거려주었다. 공수특전단의 만행을 보았을 때 인간에 대한 절망을 맛보았음에도 결코 사라질 수 없는, 인간에 대한 신뢰와 사랑을 지금 그녀는 분명히 확인하는 것이었다.

더 가까운 곳에서 연발총 소리가 연이어 들려왔다. 형자는 소년이 잡고 있던 총을 같이 잡았다. 김두칠은 총대를 잡고 있는 손에 힘을 주었다. 그는 망연한 밤하늘에 대고 혼잣말처럼 뇌었다.

"죽는 건 두렵지 않아요. 어디 산에 파묻히기라도 하면 다행이죠. 살이 썩으면 흙은 영양분을 얻게 되어 이름 모를 풀꽃을 피우게 할 수도 있겠죠. 재수가 좋으면 진달래를 피울 수도 있구요. 어릴 때 배고프면 산에서 진달래를 많이 따 먹었지요. 내가 죽어서 피운 진달래를 배고픈 어린애들이 따 먹으면 내가 다시 살아나는 게 아니겠어요."

like the sound of roadside trees being crunched. They could also smell a fragrance that seemed to be coming from the grass. Kim Du-chil breathed it in deeply. He murmured to himself.

"What a wonderful world..."

The soldier next to him nodded. A guy with a scar on his cheek, he had a clear and serious face. The other soldier was a boy about fifteen or sixteen years old. Perhaps because of the weight of the rifle, one of his shoulders was drooping. The boy said, "Strangely, I remember a time when I was eating dinner with my family around a table."

After a few minutes, he continued, "Then, even after I had eaten, I got hungry again as soon as I put down my spoon. But here I don't feel hungry although I eat only once a day. I feel reassured and happy about everything for no clear reason."

The boy quietly touched the barrel of his gun as if he was proud. Then, looking at Hyeong-ja, he asked, "Do you have a gun, too, Nuna?"[11]

"Yes, I do."

"You're fine, then."

They could hear the sound of magazine rifles far away. It wasn't the sound of their own troops. Hyeong-ja could tell whose side the sound was

"그래요, 죽음은 그런 걸 거예요. 살아 있는 생명들은 하나도 사라지지 않을 거예요."

형자가 말했다.

연발총 소리와 뒤섞여 대지를 짓밟는 굉음이 들려왔다. 탱크의 캐터필러[1] 소리였다. 소리는 밤의 적막을 하나하나 삼킬 듯이 지축을 천천히 뒤흔들어왔다.

도청 전체에 비상이 걸렸다. 김두칠이 M1 소총을 꽉 보듬어 안으며 소리쳤다.

"개새끼들, 본때를 보여줘야지."

시민군들은 급히 제 위치로 치달려갔다.

도청은 탱크를 앞세운 계엄군에 의해 완전히 포위되었다. 김두칠은 은폐물 뒤에 엎드려 마른침을 삼켰다. 검은 장막 속에 숫자를 헤아릴 수 없는 많은 탱크와 장갑차가 희끗희끗 보였다. 갑자기 장갑차 위에서 빛이 번쩍했다. 서치라이트였다. 칼날 같은 빛이 눈 깊숙이 파고들었다. 눈을 감고서도 한동안 망막이 아른거렸다. 김두칠은 깊은 물속에 잠기는 것처럼 공포가 확 밀려왔다. 앞을 볼 수가 없어 옆으로 눈을 돌렸다. 동지들은 은폐물 뒤에서 숨소리도 없이 웅크리고 있었다. 서치라이트에 도청은 완전히

coming from. The sound from their side was a dull staccato, *tak, tak, tak.* Kim Du-chil took a cigarette from his shirt pocket.

"You have a cigarette!" said the soldier with a scar on his face as if happy to see it.

"I could get only one cigarette from somebody."

He lit a match. It was bright for a moment. After lighting the cigarette, he handed it to the soldier with a scar.

"You smoke first."

"You smoke first."

"Please, you smoke first."

They took turns, alternating puffs. When the cigarette was burned down to its middle, Kim Du-chil offered it to the boy.

"You have a puff, too."

"I don't know how."

"Give it a try, still. This could be your last cigarette..."

The boy took it with both hands and carefully had a puff. Hyeong-ja ordinarily didn't like cigarette smoke at all, but now it was as fragrant as the smell of young skin.

"You have a puff, too, Nuna."

"I feel as if I already did."

모습을 드러내었고, 손가락 움직임조차 확연하게 보였다. 은폐물 사이 골이 팬 곳곳에 총구멍이 적들을 향해 겨눠지고 있었다. 옆의 동지가 마른침을 삼켰다. 그들은 공격 명령이 떨어질 때를 가슴 죄며 기다렸다. 총알이 부족해서 정확한 사정거리 안에 적이 들어왔을 때 총을 쏘기로 이미 약속이 되어 있었다.

계엄군은 항복 권유의 최후통첩을 방송했다.

"폭도들에게 경고한다. 너희들은 현재 완전히 포위되었다. 열 셀 때까지 무기를 버리고 투항하라."

하나.

김두칠은 총을 서치라이트 쪽으로 조준했다.

두울.

숨 막히는 순간, 총을 잡고 있는 손에 힘을 주었다.

세엣.

네엣.

그때 도청 본관 창문에서 한 시민군의 목소리가 잠시의 정적을 찢었다.

"개자식들아."

동시에 총소리가 계엄군의 서치라이트를 박살내었다. 주위는 다시 캄캄해졌다. 동지들과 더불어 김두칠은 방아

Hyeong-ja suddenly felt as if they were her long lost brothers. She blinked, feeling she was about to tear up again. Kim Du-chil gently patted her several times on the shoulder. Although she despaired of human beings when she saw the brutalities committed by the airborne troops, this moment confirmed her undying love for, and trust in, people.

The sound of magazine rifles was drawing nearer. Hyeong-ja and the boy held his rifle together. Kim Du-chil clutched his gun barrel more tightly. He muttered towards the vast night sky, "I'm not afraid of dying. I'd be lucky if I get buried on some mountain. If my flesh rots, the soil will get nutrients to help nameless flowers bloom. If I get really lucky, I could even make azaleas bloom. When I was young and hungry, I ate azaleas many times. If hungry children eat the azaleas I make bloom, I'll be alive again."

"Yes, that's what death must be. No lives simply disappear," said Hyeong-ja.

Together with the sound of magazine rifles, a roaring was approaching. It was the sound of tank treads trampling the earth. The sound slowly shook the ground, as if swallowing the silence of the night one inch at a time.

쇠를 당겼다. 계엄군의 일제사격이 개시되었다. 그들의 자동화기가 콩 볶는 소리를 내며 일시에 퍼부어 왔다. 김두칠은 달려오는 수많은 군홧발을 보았다. 계속 방아쇠를 당겼다. 총탄 하나가 날아와 김두칠의 어깨에 파고들었다. 은폐물 뒤로 나동그라졌다. 동지들도 피를 흘리며 쓰러져 있었다. 군홧발은 마치 대지를 뒤흔드는 것같이 은폐물 위를 넘어 그들을 밟고 지나갔다. 김두칠은 기를 쓰고 몸을 일으키려고 애써 보았다. 가까스로 손 한쪽을 은폐물 위에 올려놓았다. 온 힘을 다해 상체를 일으켰다. 그는 총을 은폐물 위에 올려놓았다. 아까보다 더 많은 군홧발이 몰려들고 있었다. 여러 발의 총탄이 천지를 흔들었다. 김두칠은 은폐물 위로 몸을 늘어뜨렸다. 총은 가슴께에 품고 있었다. 부릅뜬 두 눈이 먼 곳을 응시하였다. 두 눈은 군홧발을 넘어, 탱크와 장갑차를 넘어, 쭉 뻗은 시가지를 넘어 먼 곳 고향 산천을 바라보고 있었다.

어머니!

입속에서 나오는 마지막 부르짖음이 총성과 군홧발 소리에 묻혀버렸다.

The entire complex was put on emergency alert. Hugging his M1 rifle, Kim Du-chil shouted, "Sons of bitches, I'll teach you a lesson!"

Citizen soldiers rushed to their posts.

The complex was completely surrounded by the martial law enforcement troops. Kim Du-chil hunkered down behind a barricade with bated breath. Behind the black curtain, innumerable tanks and armed motorcars were barely visible. Suddenly, something flashed from the top of a motorcar. It was a searchlight. A sharp light was digging deeply into his eyes like the blade of a knife. Even with his eyes closed, the light kept flickering on his retina. Fear overtook Kim Du-chil in an instant as if he was being submerged in deep water. Because he couldn't see in front of him, he glanced to the side. Fellow citizen soldiers were crouching behind barricades, holding their breaths. The building complex stood bare under the searchlight. It was so clear you could even see people's fingers moving. Muzzles of guns were aiming at the enemy from gaps in the barricades. The fellow next to him was swallowing with a dry mouth. They were anxiously waiting for the signal to attack. They had decided to wait until

3

　어머니는 한물간 딸기를 받아와 리어카에 끌고 나다녔
다. 딸기철은 이미 지나 잼감으로나 적당했지만, 싼값에
도 잘 팔려나가지 않았다. 어머니가 투덜거렸다.

　"난리를 겪고 난 후라 잼도 안 만드는가 보다. 빨리 토
마토가 익어야 될 텐데……"

　어머니는 아무 일도 없었다는 듯 먹고사는 일에 매달렸
다. 동생들은 학교에 나가기 시작했고, 사람들은 일상을
살아가기 시작했다. 청소차는 격일제로 딸랑거리며 나타
났고, 아낙네들은 마당에 물을 휙휙 뿌리며 집 안을 말끔
하게 청소하기도 했다. 어린아이들은 전쟁놀이를 신나게
해댔고, 로봇이니 마징가제트니 하는 장난감들은 뒷전으
로 내팽개쳐 버렸다.

　순분은 이 모든 일이 비현실적으로 보이기도 하였고 또
놀랍기도 하였다. 그녀로서는 어떻게 시작하여야 할지를
몰랐다. 방구석에 멍하니 틀어박혀 죽은 듯이 누워 있었
다. 보다 못해 어머니가 역정을 냈다.

　"이것아, 정신 차리고 먹고살 생각을 해야지. 누워만 있
으면 밥이 들어오냐, 떡이 들어오냐."

the enemy came within range before they began shooting, because they were short of bullets.

The martial law enforcement troops were broadcasting an ultimatum, urging them to surrender.

"We warn you mobsters. You're completely surrounded. Drop your arms and surrender before I finish counting to ten."

One.

Kim Du-chil aimed his gun at the searchlight.

Two-o.

Holding his breath, he held his rifle tighter.

Three-ee.

Fo-o-u-u-r.

At that moment the shout of a citizen soldier from a window in the main building of the complex tore the momentary silence.

"You, sons-of-bitches!"

Simultaneously, a gunshot shattered the searchlight of the martial law enforcement troops. It was pitch black again. Kim Du-chil pulled the trigger side-by-side with his fellow citizen soldiers. The troops opened up with a volley. In an instant, their automatic weapons started popping like roasting beans. Kim Du-chil saw numerous combat boots running towards the building. He kept on pulling

동생들의 2기분 납부금 고지서가 날아들어 온 지도 꽤 되었다. 순분은 도리 없이 공장엘 나가기 시작했다. 어쩌다 도청 앞에 멈춘 적이 있었다. 분수대에선 물줄기가 뿜어 올랐고 화려한 꽃장식이 물기를 머금어 반짝거렸다. 도청 안 그녀가 머물렀던 곳에 시선이 멈추자 걷잡을 수 없는 눈물이 솟구쳤다. 도망치듯 그곳을 빠져나왔다. 그 후로 도청 앞을 피해서 다녔다. 공장에서 일하는 시간이 오히려 마음이 편하기도 하였다. 예비종이 울리고 작업장에 들어서 조례를 마치면 그때부터 그녀는 한낱 기계에 지나지 않았다. 시끄러운 기계 소리와 밝은 형광등 불빛을 동무 삼아 야간작업도 부지런히 해냈다. 전번 사태로 1억인가가 손해났다고 사장은 입을 쩝쩝 다셨다. 마치 근로자들에게 죄가 있는 양 몰아붙였다. 졸리면 타이밍[2]과 박카스를 사먹었다.

　야학은 폐쇄되었다. 전국적으로 야학이 탄압 국면을 맞았다. 야학을 엮어 무슨 사건을 조작하려는 분위기가 팽배했다. 근로자들은 그나마 공부할 기회도 빼앗겨 버렸다. 일요 예배 때에 이따금 강학들 얼굴이 보였다. 윤강일은 나타나지 않았다. 강학들은 목사가 안 볼 때 찬송가 대신 유행가를 불렀다. 「보고 싶은 얼굴」. 이 유행가가 대학

the trigger. A bullet flew deeply into his shoulder. He tumbled down behind the barricade. Other fellow citizen soldiers were lying on the floor bleeding. Military boots jumped over the barricades and stepped all over their bodies with earthshaking force. Kim Du-chil tried with all his might to get up. He finally managed to put one hand on top of the barricade. With all of his remaining strength, he lifted his upper body. He put his rifle on top of the barricade. Even more military boots came storming in. Many shots were shaking the air. Kim Du-chil slouched down on the barricade. He was hugging his rifle in his arms. His fiercely glaring eyes were staring far away. They were looking at the mountains and rivers of his home village, beyond the military boots, beyond the tanks and armored motorcars, beyond the wide, straight city streets.

"Mother!"

His last cry was buried under the thundering of shots and military boots.

3

Mother bought out-of-season strawberries and sold them from a pushcart. Because they were out of

가에서 불리고 있다고 했다. 순분이들은 절대 이 노래를 따라 부르지 않았다. 그녀들은 내밀한 부분을 싸안아 가슴 한 귀퉁이에 꼭꼭 숨겨두고 있었다. 내밀한 부분들을 내비치는 동료가 있으면 화를 버럭 냈다. 가령 형자 얘기가 나온다든가, 마지막 도청을 빠져나오던 장면, 또는 궐기대회에서 외쳤던 여러 구호의 용어들…… 순분이들은 서로에게 분노했고 증오까지 하였다. 상대방에 대해서 조금도 너그럽지 못했다. 생각을 해보면 자기 자신에 대한 분노가 상대방에게 칼을 들이대는 것 같았다.

신문에서는 폭도들의 이름이 게재되었고 마치 커다란 범죄 조직을 터뜨리는 것 같았다. 폭도들이 수감되어 있는 상무관은 공기조차 얼어붙어 있는 것 같았다. 마지막 도청 안에도 살아남은 자가 있다는 소식이 들려왔을 때 순분이들은 혹시나 하고 상무관 쪽으로 가보았다. 카키색3) 만 보아도 깜짝깜짝 놀라는 무서움을 간신히 가라앉히고 정문으로 다가갔다. 순분이가 얼어붙은 입을 떼었다.

"저…… 사람을 찾는데요."

"어떤 사람?"

군인이 눈을 치켜들었다.

"언닌데……"

season, they were fit for making jam, but they weren't selling very well, although they were cheap. Mother complained, "I guess people aren't even making jam after the war. I hope the tomatoes ripen soon..."

Mother had jumped into supporting her family as if nothing had happened. Sunbun's younger siblings went back to school, and people began living their ordinary lives again. The garbage truck appeared every other day, ringing its bells, and women scrubbed their houses and sprinkled their yards with water. Children played excitedly at soldiers, abandoning toys like robots and Mazinger Z's.

Sunbun found all of this unreal and shocking. She didn't know how to begin. Shutting herself up in a corner of her room, she stayed in bed like a corpse. Unable to stand it any longer, Mother burst into a rage.

"Hey, you, pull yourself together and go support your family. If all you do is lie around, will rice or a rice cake enter your mouth by itself?"

It had been a while since her younger siblings' tuition bills had been delivered. Sunbun had to begin to work at the factory. Once she happened to stop in front of the governor's office building com-

"폭도 동생이 왔구먼."

군인의 눈빛이 날카로워졌다. 그녀들은 더 이상 물어보지도 못하고 도망치듯 빠져나왔다.

상무관을 갔다온 후로 그녀들은 더욱더 상대방에 대해 불만을 갖게 되었다. 둘이 모이면 딴 친구 욕을 해댔다. 딴 친구는 이쪽 욕을 했다.

"사람다운 사람은 하나도 안 남았어." 하고 철순이가 내뱉으면,

"넌 사람답니?"

하고 미숙이가 앙칼지게 되물었다. 영순이가 모 인권 단체에서 온 목사에게 도청 안에 있었던 사건들을 이야기할 때였다. 철순이가 영순이를 제지하며 말했다.

"넌 제일 먼저 빠져나갔어. 넌 말할 자격이 없어."

영순이가 울음을 터뜨렸다. 목사가 고개를 갸웃거리며 말했다.

"그런 엄청난 일을 겪고도 왜 서로 헐뜯습니까? 지금은 화해를 할 땝니다."

"화해라고요?"

미숙이의 목소리가 뾰족해졌다. 신문에서나 인권 단체, 종교 단체, 어디에서나 화해라는 말이 많이 떠돌았다. 용

plex. Streams of water were sprouting upward from the fountain, and splendid floral decorations were sparkling beneath. When her eyes drifted to that place she had been, they were filled with tears. She had left there as if running away. Since then, she avoided passing by the building. In a way, she felt better working in the factory. After the warning bell, she entered the workshop, attended the morning meeting, and became a mere machine. Befriending machine noise and intense fluorescent light, she worked diligently at night as well. The owner clucked his tongue, complaining that he had lost something like a hundred million *won* because of the recent incident. He upbraided the workers as if they were to blame. When she was sleepy, she took a Timing or a Bacchus to stay awake.[12]

The night school was closed. Night schools were suppressed all over the country. It seemed that the government was trying to fabricate some conspiracy that would implicate all the night schools. Workers lost even that small opportunity to study. She occasionally saw a few night school teachers during Sunday services. Yun Gang-il never showed up. Night school teachers sang popular songs instead of hymns when the priest wasn't around. "Faces I

서라는 용어도 뒤따랐다. 정부에서는 화해와 용서의 뜻으로 폭도들에게 사형은 처하지 않는다고 발표하였다. 화해와 용서라는 말 속에는 진상을 가리려는 음모의 냄새가 풍겼다. 그녀들은 절대로 화해할 수 없었다. 그 누구와 화해할 수 없다는 말인가. 군사 독재 정권일 수도 있고, 폭도라고 떠드는 언론, 살아남은 자들 그리고 자기 자신일 수도 있었다. 군사 독재 정권, 언론, 살아남은 자들은 저 멀리에 있었고 가장 구체적으로 맞닿은 것은 자기 자신과 동료들이었다. 그녀들은 자신을 할퀴고 상대방을 할퀴고, 상처 난 부분에 피가 흐르고, 피가 흐른 부분이 채 아물기도 전에 다시 칼을 꽂았다. 그리하여 더 이상 혼자서 감추어 두었던 내밀한 부분마저 찢겨져 나와 아무것도 감출 것이 없었다. 그것은 마치 대검으로 찔리어 내장이 길 위에 삐져나와, 좀 전에 먹었던 밥알이 햇빛에 선명히 드러난 것 같았다. 그녀들은 눈을 똑바로 뜨고 진단하지 않을 수 없었다. 살아 있는 것은 부끄러운 일이었다. 그녀들은 비로소 살아 있는 것에 정당성을 부여해왔던 자신들의 내밀한 부분을 여지없이 부수어버릴 수밖에 없었다.

살아 있는 것은 개인의 선택이었고 하늘 우러러 한 점 부끄러움이었고, 비겁이었고 또한 죄악이었다. 그것을 인

Miss"—people said this popular song was sung a lot on college campuses. Sunbun and her friends never sang it. They were hiding their innermost feelings deep inside tiny corners of their hearts. If anybody happened to reveal her inner feelings, the others flew into a rage. For example, if anybody mentioned the name Hyeong-ja, the fact that they left the governor's office building complex, or various rally slogans, Sunbun and her friends became angry with each other, almost to the point of hatred. They weren't considerate. In retrospect, they must have turned their anger at themselves into a knife thrusts at each other.

Newspapers published the names of the "rebels" as if they belonged to a large criminal organization. In the Sangmu building where the "rebels" were imprisoned, even the air seemed frozen. When Sunbun and her friends heard that there were survivors from the governor's office building complex, they hurried to the Sangmu building. After barely suppressing their fear that could be triggered by the sight of khaki, they approached the main gate. Sunbun opened her frozen mouth, "Mmm... We're here to look for someone."

"Whom?"

정해야만 했다. 그리고 다시 시작할 것이었다.

이튿날부터 틈이 나는 대로 사망자와 부상자들을 찾아
다녔다. 순분이 동네에서만도 다섯 명의 사망자와 일곱
명의 부상자가 있었다. 그녀들이 확인해볼 수 있는 대상
은 한정된 것이었다. 인권 단체들을 쫓아다녔다. 기독교
연합회와 가톨릭센터, 5·18광주의거유족회, 5·18부상자
동지회 등등이었다. 부상자 신원 확인은 722명 정도였고
구속자는 421명이 확인되었다. 사망자는 망월동에 묻힌
200여 구가 못 되는 숫자와 인권 단체들이 확인한 400여
구 이외에는 신원이 드러나지 않았다. 2,000여 명이 죽었
을 거라는 풍문이 나돌았다. 그 숫자보다 더 많으면 많았
지 적지는 않을 것이었다. 순분이 동네에서 죽은 다섯 명
의 사망자 중에서 두 명만이 인권 단체에 등록하였다. 딴
가족들은 쉬쉬하며 등록하기를 한사코 거부하였다. 그때
살벌한 분위기로는 그럴 수밖에 없었다. 언론에서는 계속
폭도니 불순분자니 하고 몰아붙이고 있었고 신고한다는
것은 대역죄를 지은 가정이 된다는 것을 의미했다.

그녀들은 부상자와 구속자 명단을 놓고 계급적으로 분
류해보았다. 사망자는 제외했다. 잘못 알려지면 그 숫자
만 죽었다고 확정될 수 있으니 말이다. 사망자는 좋은 세

The soldier glared.

"My sister..."

"So, you must be a rebel's sister!"

His eyes became harsh. They couldn't persevere, and left as if running away again.

After that visit, they became even more dissatisfied with each other. When two of them got together, they cursed the others. Meanwhile, the others were cursing them somewhere else.

"All the real human beings are gone."

When Cheol-sun spat that out, Misuk retorted sharply, "So, are you a real human being?"

Once Yeong-sun was in the middle of telling a priest from a human rights organization what had happened in the governor's office building complex. Cheol-sun interrupted her and said, "You left first. You have no right to talk about it."

Yeong-sun burst into tears. The priest, slowly shaking his head sideways, said, "Why are you blaming each other after such a terrible incident? Now is the time to reconcile."

"Reconcile?"

Misuk's voice was sharp. People were talking about reconciliation everywhere—in newspapers, human rights organizations, and religious organiza-

상이 오면 정확히 확인해야 될 일이었다.

유산자 계급—엄밀한 의미에서 이 계급의 사람은 한 사람도 없다. 그러나 안정된 직업을 가진 사람들을 이 계급에 포함시켰다. 회사원, 축산업, 공무원 등등.

지식인 계급—재야 인사, 운동권 청년, 교사, 대학생, 학생, 지적인 일에 종사하는 사람들 등등.

농민 계급—농업에 종사하는 모든 사람들.

무산자 계급—세 곳에 포함되지 않은 모든 사람들을 이 계급에 집어넣었다. 공원, 세차공, 음식점 배달원, 무직, 외판원, 타일공, 양복공, 세탁공, 청소부, 노점상, 점원, 가난한 주부, 운전수, 보일러공, 소상인, 막노동, 고물상, 행상, 용접공, 자개공, 목공, 구두닦이 등등.

유산자 계급—34명

지식인 계급—240명

농민 계급—47명

무산자 계급—822명

대략 71퍼센트가 무산자 계급이었다. 지식인 계급에 속하는 대부분의 숫자는 예비 검속으로 붙잡혀 간 사람들이었다. 붙잡혀 가지 않았다면 모두 투쟁에 가담했을까. 대

tions. The term "forgiveness," followed, too. Government announced that they wouldn't execute the rebels for the sake of reconciliation and forgiveness. Terms like "reconciliation" and "forgiveness" reeked of a conspiracy to hide the truth. Sunbun and her friends didn't feel they could ever reconcile. With whom couldn't they reconcile? The military dictatorship and the press that were calling them mobsters, the survivors, or themselves? The military government, the press, and the survivors were all far away, while their friends were nearby and concrete. They scratched harshly at themselves and each other, plunging knives into their bloody unhealed wounds. In the end, even the innermost feelings they tried to keep hidden were exposed, and they had nothing more to hide. It was as if grains of rice eaten only a little while earlier were vividly revealed in the sunlight as a person's intestines spilled across the road after his belly had been cut open by a bayonet. They had to open their eyes and think about themselves. It was shameful to be alive. They had to finally destroy their innermost secret, i.e. the fact that they had been trying to justify still being alive.

They chose to live, which was "a spot of shame under the sky," cowardice, and sin.[13] They had to

답은 미지수이지만 운 좋게 검거를 모면한 사람들의 행동을 기준해본다면 가정은 나온다. 많은 사람들이 투쟁에서 이탈했을 것이다. 그렇다면 무산자 계급의 퍼센트는 더 높아질 것이다. 80퍼센트, 90퍼센트. 결과를 놓고 보니 순분은 형자의 말이 새삼 떠올랐다. 그녀가 동료들에게 말했다.

"언니가 왜 그랬는지 이제야 알겠어."

"뭐라고 그랬는데?"

철순이가 눈을 빛내며 물었다. 영순이, 미숙이도 순분이를 주시했다.

"그때 언니가 말했어."

순분은 말을 끊었다. 되살아난 듯 형자의 모습이 생생했다. 그때 바람에 머리카락이 나부꼈지. 금남로에 불빛이 빛나기 시작했고 새 떼들이 분수대 위를 빙빙 돌았지. 그리고 도청의 창문들. 언니는 가슴속에 꼭꼭 담아두려는 듯 하나하나 시선을 주었지. 삶의 소중함을 나타내는 눈빛이 있다면 그때 언니의 눈빛이 그러했어. 그 모두를 아는 자만이 죽음도 확고하게 받아들이는 것일까. 언니가 말했지.

"어떤 사람들이 이 항쟁에 가담했고 투쟁했고 죽었는가

acknowledge this to start over.

From the next day on, they visited the dead and wounded whenever they could. There were no fewer than five dead and seven wounded in Sunbun's neighborhood alone. The number of people whose death or injury they could directly confirm was very limited. They visited human rights organizations such as the Christian Council of Korea, the Catholic Center, the Association of Bereaved Families of May Eighteenth Gwangju Revolution, and the Association of Wounded Comrades of the May Eighteenth. The number of the confirmed injured was around seven hundred twenty-two and of the confirmed detained, four hundred twenty-one. As for the dead, they couldn't confirm their identities beyond the fewer than two hundred buried in the Mangwol-dong Cemetery and four hundred more confirmed by human rights organizations. There were rumors that there had been over two thousand deaths. So the number of the dead could be greater than, but definitely not fewer than, two thousand. Of the five deaths from Sunbun's neighborhood, only two were registered at the human rights organizations. Other families kept quiet their dead and insisted on not registering

를 꼭 기억해야 돼. 그러면 너희들은 알게 될 거야. 어떤 사람들이 역사를 만들어 가는가를…… 그것은 곧 너희들의 힘이 될 거야."

그녀들은 말없이 앉아 있었다. 순분은 무산자 계급의 퍼센트에 시선을 고정시키고 있었다. 도청에서 보았던 많은 사람들이 주마등처럼 떠올랐다. 말없이 눈만 번쩍이던 사람, 턱에 칼자국이 있던 사람, 거친 욕을 끊임없이 해대던 사람, 몸집은 작은데 손이 유난히 컸던 사람, 밥을 먹으면서도 총만은 거머쥐고 있던 사람, 해맑은 어린 사람, 사람들. 그리고 김두칠과 형자. 각양각색의 사람들. 그러나 하나다. 모두가 없는 사람들이다.

"너희들도 보았지?"

자신의 생각 속에 떠오른 물음을 순분은 물었다. 철순이가 되물었다.

"뭘?"

"그때 있었던 사람들…… 마지막 밤 도청에 있었던 사람들 말야. 그날 저녁 즈음에 계엄군이 쳐들어올 것을 다 알고 있었잖아."

"마지막 궐기대회 때 이미 예상되고 있었지."

영순이가 말했다.

them. This was understandable, given the brutal environment of the time. The press continued to accuse the dead of being mobsters and "impure elements." So, if a family registered its member as dead, this meant acknowledging that he or she had committed high treason.

Sunbun and her friends also tried to categorize the wounded and detained by social class. They didn't include the dead, concerned that if others learned the number they were using, it might be taken for the actual number of the dead. They felt that the real number of the dead should be determined accurately in the future, when things had improved in the outside world.

Have—strictly speaking, nobody in this class was wounded or detained: but they also included those with secure jobs, like white-collar workers, stock-breeders, and government employees

Intellectuals—distinguished men out of office, young activists, teachers, college students, other students, and other people doing intellectual work

Peasant class—all farmers

Have-nots—they included in this class all those who didn't belong to the other three categories; factory workers, car washers, restaurant delivery boys,

"그런데도 사람들은 돌아갔어. 도청과 몇몇 건물을 지키던 사람들과 외곽 지대를 방어하던 시민군들만 빼놓고……"

마음속에 있는 말이 잘 나오지 않는 듯 순분은 침을 꿀꺽 삼켰다. 그녀의 시선이 동료들을 넘어 먼 곳을 바라보았다. 이마에 가느다란 선이 나타났다. 다시 시선이 돌아오면서 입을 떼었다.

"우리가 죽을 줄 알면서도 사람들은 돌아갔어."

"마지막엔 참 외로웠지."

미숙이가 쉰 듯한 목소리로 말했다. 영순이가 말을 이었다.

"모든 사람들이 도청 광장에 집결하고 버텼으면 하는 생각도 들었어. 그렇다면 제아무리 계엄군이라도 쳐들어올 수 있었겠어?"

"그때 궐기대회의 열기로 보아서는 그럴 수도 있을 것 같았는데 말야."

철순이가 말했다. 미숙이의 눈빛이 흐려왔다. 그녀는 가라앉은 목소리로 말하기 시작했다.

"결국 도청이나 외곽 방어를 위해서 죽은 사람들만이 남았을 뿐이야. 대부분이 없는 사람들이고."

the unemployed, salesmen, tile workers, tailors, launders, street sweepers, stall keepers, sales people, poor housewives, drivers, plumbers, small merchants, day laborers, dealers in secondhand, peddlers, welders, shell workers, carpenters, shoe shines, etc.

Haves—34
Intellectuals—240
Peasants—47
Have-nots—822

Around 71% belonged to the class of have-nots. Most of the intellectuals were those who had been taken into preliminary custody. Would they have participated in the fight if they hadn't already been detained? There was no way to know the answer, but one could presume it, based on the actions of those who luckily escaped preliminary custody. Many would have left the scene of the fighting. If so, the percentage of have-nots would be even higher—80 or 90%. Looking at this result, Sunbun was reminded of Hyeong-ja's words and said to her friends, "Now I can understand what Hyeong-ja meant."

"투쟁이란 과연 무엇일까?"

순분이가 자문하듯 물었다. 턱에 손을 고이고 있던 영순이가 생각할 겨를도 없이 대답했다.

"형자 언니같이 행동하는 거지."

"그래, 끝까지 책임지는 것만이 투쟁이라고 말할 수 있어." 하면서 순분은 손가락으로 이마를 짚었다. 생각을 모으는 듯했다. 영순이가 작은 목소리로 말했다.

"미국이라는 정체를 이번에 분명히 알았어."

"정체고 나발이고 미국은 적이야. 형자 언니가 죽었잖아. 도청 함락은 미국의 동의하에 이루어진 것이니까."

철순이가 흥분된 어조로 말하자 영순이, 미숙이도 흥분해서 말을 거들었다.

계속 조용히 있는 순분이를 보며 한참 만에야 세 사람은 서로 눈짓을 했다. 영순이가 순분이 들으라는 듯 한마디 했다.

"아유, 배고파. 열 시가 넘었잖아."

그제서야 순분은 동료들을 바라보며 말했다.

"시간이 벌써 그렇게 됐니? 이제 일어나야겠구나."

미숙이는 그대로 앉아 있었다. 영순이가 그녀의 팔을 잡아 일으키며 말했다.

"What did she say?" asked Cheol-sun, her eyes shining. Yeong-sun and Misuk also watched Sunbun attentively.

"She told me at the time..."

Sunbun stopped. She could vividly see Hyeong-ja before her, as if she had come back from the dead. Her hair was fluttering in the breeze. Lights were turning on one after another on Geumnam-ro Street, and birds were circling above the fountain. And then the windows of the governor's office building complex... 'Eonni looked at them one by one. It looked as if she wanted to cherish them in her heart. If eyes could show how precious life is, her eyes did. Maybe only those who understand this accept death resolutely?'

"Eonni said to me, 'you must remember who participated, fought, and died in this struggle. Then, you'll know who makes history... That knowledge will make you stronger.'"

They sat silently. Sunbun's eyes were fixed on the number showing the percentage of have-nots wounded or detained. Faces of people she had seen in the governor's office building quickly appeared before her one by one. A silent person with bright eyes, one with a scar on his chin, one with a foul

"넌 안 갈래?"

"응…… 저 말야."

말끝을 흐렸다. 순분이가 물었다.

"뭐 할 말이 남았니?"

"응…… 그냥, 아니 사실은……" 하고 또 말끝을 흐렸다. 철순이와 미숙이의 눈길이 부딪쳤다. 그녀들은 당황스러운 기색을 감추려는 듯 부산스럽게 일어났다.

순분은 버스표를 꺼냈다. 버스가 오고 있었다. 막 정차를 하는데 미숙이가 순분의 팔을 잡아끌었다. 버스는 가버렸다. 미숙이가 목소리를 낮추어 말했다.

"모두 우리 자취방에 가자."

"왜?"

"윤 선생님이 오기로 했어."

"잠수함 탔잖아."

"그러니까 오는 거지."

미숙이와 철순이는 발산다리 너머 달동네에 월세방을 얻어 자취하고 있었다.

mouth, a small person with large hands, one holding his rifle even while he was eating, and a fair-skinned young boy... Then, Kim Du-chil and Hyeong-ja. All kinds of people... But they were one. They were all have-nots.

"You've all seen them, haven't you?"

Sunbun asked as if her friends had been listening to her thoughts. Cheol-sun asked her back, "What?"

"Those people who were there... Those who remained in the governor's office building complex the last night... They all knew that the martial law troops would attack that night, didn't they?"

"It was already known during the last rally," said Yeong-sun.

"Nevertheless, people went home. Except for those defending the governor's office building complex and a few other buildings and those defending the outskirts..."

As if she couldn't bring herself to say it, Sunbun swallowed. She looked far off, beyond her friends. A thin crease appeared on her forehead. Her gaze returned and she spoke again.

"People went home, knowing that we would all die."

"We were so alone then," said Misuk, hoarsely.

발바리가 꼬리를 치다가 순분이 영순이를 보고 캥캥 짖
었다. 그 소리에 옆방 아이가 깨어났는지 칭얼거렸다. 방
한 칸에 부엌이 딸린 방들이 네 개나 있었다. 처마 밑을
잇대어 선라이트[4]로 얼기설기 엮어놓은 부엌으로 그녀들
은 몰려들어 갔다. 그릇을 얹어놓은 선반 하나가 달려 있
었다. 선반 가운데에 작은 종지가 엎어져 있었다. 미숙은
종지를 살짝 들었다. 열쇠가 있었다. 방문을 열었다. 이불
을 얹어 놓은 나무 궤짝, 벽에 걸려 있는 옷 나부랭이들,
한 귀퉁이에 조그만 책꽂이, 책꽂이 위쪽 벽에는 누르스
름한 한지에 칼로 오려내듯이 단호하게 검정으로 각인된
판화가 액자도 없이 붙어 있었다. 노동자가 한 손엔 밥그
릇을, 또 한 손엔 『근로기준법』이라고 쓴 책을 들고 있었
다. 불타는 눈물이 아니라 불타는 몸을 나타내듯 불꽃이
화면 가득히 타오르는 그림이었다. 그 노동자는 전태일이
었다.

그녀들은 오면서 사온 라면을 끓여 먹었다. 김치도 없
었다.

"애, 김치 좀 담가 먹어라. 기집애가 게을러서……"

영순이가 퉁방울을 주자 순분이도 거들었다.

"시집가면 소박맞을 일이야."

Yeong-sun continued, "I was hoping that everyone would gather in the square in front of the building and stand firm. If that had happened, could the troops even have attacked?"

"Given the enthusiasm during the rally, we could have done that," said Cheol-sun.

Misuk's eyes misted over. She began to say, calmly, "In the end, only those who died defending the governor's office building complex and the outskirts remained. Most of them were have-nots."

"What is a fight, I wonder?" asked Sunbun as if speaking to herself.

Yeong-sun who was supporting her chin with her hand said without skipping a beat, "It's acting like Hyeong-ja Eonni."

"That's right. Only being responsible until the end should be called a fight," Sunbun put her fingers on her forehead. She seemed to gather her thoughts.

Yeong-sun said in a low voice, "I learned about America very clearly through this incident."

"Whatever America is, one thing that's clear is that it is our enemy. Hyeong-ja Eonni died. The fall of the governor's office building complex couldn't have happened without American consent," Cheol-sun said excitedly, and Yeong-sun and Misuk, also

그녀들은 제각기 편한 자세로 누웠다. 넷이 누우니 발 디딜 틈도 없었다. 그중 몸이 통통한 영순이가 세 사람의 눈총을 받았다.

"필요 없이 살찌는 것도 죄가 된다는 거, 너희들 지금 보았지?" 하면서 미숙이가 킥킥 웃었다. 골목으로 면해 있는 창밖으로 술 취한 남자의 흥얼거리는 노랫소리가 들려왔다. 노랫소리가 멀어지면서 두 남녀의 목소리가 들려왔다.

"수입이 괜찮았어?"

"괜찮긴, 순경한테 쫓겨다니느라고 혼쭐만 났어."

"곧 겨울이 닥쳐올 텐데……"

목소리가 멀어지면서 한동안 잠잠했다.

창문에서 톡톡, 소리가 났다. 미숙이가 일어나 창문 밖을 내다보았다. 흐릿한 불빛 속에 윤강일이 서 있었다. 창문을 조금 열고 미숙이가 속삭이듯 말했다.

"거기 가만히 계세요."

미숙은 방문을 열고 마당으로 나갔다. 이 방 저 방으로 귀를 기울였다. 조용했다. 발바리가 귀를 쫑긋거렸다. 발바리를 안고 대문을 열었다. 그림자처럼 윤강일이 들어섰다. 그는 발걸음을 죽이며 부엌으로 들어갔다. 미숙은 대

excited, agreed.

Realizing after a while that Sunbun remained silent, the three exchanged glances. Yeong-sun said as if to Sunbun, "Jeez, I'm hungry. It's past ten."

At this, Sunbun finally looked at them and said, "Really? Let's go."

Misuk kept sitting where she was. Pulling her by the arms, Yeong-sun asked, "Aren't you coming?"

"Well... By the way..." She didn't finish her sentence.

Sunbun asked, "What? Do you have more to say?"

"Well... no, no, to tell you the truth..." but she didn't continue.

Cheol-sun and Misuk exchanged glances. As if they wanted to hide their embarrassments, they hurried to get up.

Sunbun took out her bus ticket. A bus was approaching. When it was about to stop, Misuk pulled Sunbun toward her. The bus passed. Misuk said in a low voice, "Let's all go to our room."

"Why?"

"Teacher Yun is supposed to come."

"Didn't he go underground?"

"That's why."

Misuk and Cheol-sun were living together in a

문 밖을 휘둘러보았다. 아무도 없다. 문을 잠그고 발바리를 놓아주었다. 부엌에서 미숙이가 물었다.

"선생님, 저녁 하셨어요?"

"대충 했어. 신경 쓰지 말고 어서 들어와."

미숙은 대접할 것이 없나 하고 이리저리 둘러보았다. 어머니가 보내준 콩 볶은 것이 생각나 쟁반에 받쳐들고 방으로 들어갔다. 윤강일의 얼굴이 초췌해 보였다. 감옥 얘기 할 때의 그 불타던 눈빛도 많이 흐려 있었다. 그가 한 사람 한 사람 둘러보고 나서 말했다.

"너희들은 여전하구나."

윤강일은 비닐봉다리를 내놓았다. 소주와 쥐포였다. 종이컵에 한잔씩 돌아가며 마셨다. 그는 계속 마셨다. 그가 말했다.

"야학은 문 닫았지?"

"네."

영순이가 대답했다.

"당분간 강경으로 나갈 것 같아." 하면서 윤강일은 깊은 한숨을 내쉬었다.

미숙이가 물었다.

"그동안 어디 계셨어요?"

rented room in a Moon village across the Balsan Bridge.[14)]

A spaniel wagged its tail and barked, on seeing Sunbun and Yeong-sun. That sound must have woken up the child in the next room, who began whining. There were four rooms with attached kitchens in the house. They entered the kitchen surrounded by woven patches of sunlight, which were connected to the eaves as well. There was a tiny bowl upside down on a shelf. Misuk gently lifted it. There was a key. She opened the door to her room. In the room, there was a wooden box, on which a folded blanket was laid, clothes hanging on the wall, a small bookcase in a corner, and an unframed print of a bold black figure on yellowish rice paper on the wall above the bookcase, a figure that looked as if it had been carved by a knife. In the print, a laborer was holding a rice bowl in one hand and the book *Labor Standard Act* in the other. It was a picture covered with flames, as if representing a burning body rather than "burning tears." The laborer was Jeon Tae-il.

They cooked ramen noodles they bought on their way home. They didn't even have kimchi.

"여기저기, 주로 서울이지만. 그곳은 확실히 언더[5]의 문화가 형성된 것 같아. 나름대로 숨 트일 곳도 있고. 여긴 완전히 깜깜절벽이구나. 사람도 없고. 사람이 없으니 도시가 텅 빈 것 같다."

"사람이 없다니요?"

철순이가 물었다.

"글쎄, 쓸 만한 사람들은 감방에 들어갔거나 잠수함 탔거나 죽었거나 했잖아."

"죽은 사람은 어떤 사람을 말하는 거예요?"

영순이가 물었다.

"상원이가 죽었잖아."

"그 외에 어떤 사람들이 죽었는지 아세요?"

순분이의 물음에 윤강일은 고개를 저었다. 순분이가 계속해서 말했다.

"죽음조차도 윤 선생님 쪽의 사람만 부상하는군요."

"무슨 뜻이지?"

아무도 대답하지 않았다. 바람에 유리창이 흔들거렸다. 윤강일은 취기가 오르는지 벽에 몸을 비스듬히 기댔다. 그가 말했다.

"야학 문 닫았다고 공부하고 담쌓으면 안 된다. 혼자서

"Make kimchi, you lazy girls!"

Yeong-sun jokingly rebuked the two, and Sunbun added, "If you were married, you'd be deserted by your husbands."

They all sprawled out in comfortable positions. There was no space left in the room after the four of them lay down. They glared at Yeong-sun, who was a bit chubby.

"Aren't we just witnessing how being unnecessarily fat is a crime?" said Misuk, giggling. A drunkard's humming was coming in through the window facing the alley. As the humming receded, they heard the voices of a man and a woman.

"Did you make good money?"

"No way. I had a hard time running away from policemen."

"Winter will be here soon..."

The voices receded and all was quiet for a while.

They could hear a *tok tok* sound coming from the window. Misuk got up and looked out. Yun Gang-il was standing below in the dim light. Opening the window a little, Misuk whispered, "Please be quiet and wait there."

Misuk opened door to her room and went out. She listened at the doors to other rooms. They were

라도 해.”

“네.”

미숙이가 대답했다.

“난 아무래도 이 도시를 다시 떠나야 할 것 같다.”

“……”

“발붙일 데도 없고 허물어진 기분이야.”

“……”

“너희들은 그렇지 않니?”

그녀들은 서로 쳐다보았다. 영순이가 말했다.

“선생님, 우린 그렇지 않아요. 할 일이 너무 많은 것 같아서……”

“어쨌든 생각을 깊게 해봐야 되겠어. 다시 시작하기 위해서 말야.”

“뭘 다시 시작해요?”

철순이가 물었다. 윤강일은 대답을 안 하고 담배를 꺼내어 불을 붙였다. 내뿜는 연기가 길다. 그의 시선이 그림에 가닿는다. 그가 말했다.

“색다른 그림인데?”

“전태일 열사예요.”

미숙이가 대답했다.

quiet. The spaniel cocked its ears. Holding it in her arms, she opened the outside door. Yun Gang-il entered like a shadow. He stepped inside the kitchen, his feet making no sound at all. Misuk looked around the street. There was nobody. She locked the door and let the spaniel go. Misuk asked in the kitchen, "Teacher, did you have dinner?"

"I had some. Don't worry and hurry in."

Misuk looked around to see if she had anything to offer. Remembering the roasted beans sent by her mother, she brought them in on a tray. Yun looked haggard. The fiery eyes he had when he talked about his prison experience were dimmed. After looking around at everyone, he said, "You all look the same."

He took a plastic bag from his jacket. There was *soju* and dried fish. They each drank a gulp of *soju* from a plastic cup. Yun kept on drinking. Then he asked, "The night school is closed, isn't it?"

"Yes," replied Yeong-sun.

"It seems that things will be tough for a while," said Yun, sighing.

Misuk asked, "Where have you been?"

"Here and there. Mostly in Seoul... It seems that a sort of underground culture was established there.

"새로운 형식이야. 예술도 달라지는 것일까."

"예술이 어떤지는 잘 모르겠고요. 이 판화를 그린 화가도 5월 항쟁에 참가했대요. 얘기하려는 것이 분명하고 값도 싸요."

미숙이가 말을 마치자 영순이가 자랑스러운 듯 말을 이었다.

"나도 있어요."

윤강일은 방 안을 둘러보다가 다시 그림에 시선을 주었다. 그가 말했다.

"이런 방에 그림이 걸려 있으니까 묘한 감동이 오는구나. 그림이 화랑이나 거실에서 뛰쳐나와 외쳐대는 것 같은 느낌이야."

모두들 그림에 시선을 주고 있었다. 불타오르는 육신이 그림에서 뛰쳐나올 것 같았다. 미숙이가 드디어 입을 열었다.

"형자 언니 소식 들으셨어요?"

"형잔 잘 있겠지?" 하면서 윤강일은 그림으로부터 시선을 떼었다. 아무도 대답하지 않았다. 그가 담배를 다 태울 때까지 말들이 없다. 술잔을 입으로 가져가는 그를 보면서 순분은 나지막이 말했다.

There were places where I could breathe. It's pitch dark here. There's nobody left, and the city feels empty since there's nobody around."

"What do you mean there's nobody around?" asked Cheol-sun.

"Well, all the decent human beings are either in prison, underground, or dead, aren't they?"

"Which dead people are you talking about?" asked Yeong-sun.

"Sang-won died, didn't he?"

"Do you know who else died?"

At Sunbun's question, Yun shook his head. Sunbun continued, "Even in death, it looks as if only your kind of people matter."

"What do you mean?"

Nobody answered. Windows were clattering at the wind. Probably feeling drunk, Yun leaned against the wall. He said, "You shouldn't give up studying just because the night school is closed. Study even if you do it by yourself!"

"Ok," answered Misuk.

"It seems that I have to leave this city."

"......"

"I have no place on which to stand, and I feel as if I have collapsed."

"언닌 죽었어요."

술잔이 잠시 허공에 머문다. 술잔이 흔들린다. 술이 조금 쏟아진다. 술잔을 내려놓는다.

"죽었다구? 언제? 어디서?"

"마지막 날 도청에서요."

윤강일은 벽에 기댄 몸을 똑바로 일으켰다. 그리고 혼잣말처럼 뇌었다.

"그 애가…… 그 애가……"

그의 손끝에서 하얗게 줄을 이루며 피어오르던 담배 연기가 흔들렸다. 그가 쉰 듯한 목소리로 물었다.

"시체는 찾았니?"

"못 찾았어요." 하고 순분은 미숙이를 바라보았다. 다시 그녀가 말했다.

"미숙이 오빠도 행불⁶⁾예요."

미숙이의 눈빛이 금시 젖어왔다. 윤강일은 입을 조금 벌리다가 이내 다물고 고개를 내려뜨렸다. 어두운 얼굴의 관자놀이에 가느다란 혈관이 파르르 떨렸다. 주먹을 쥐고 있는 손에 힘을 주었다. 이어 손을 풀면서 술잔으로 가져갔다. 연거푸 서너 잔을 마셨다. 담배를 피워 물었다. 몸도 담배 연기처럼 사그라져 가는 듯 힘없이 벽에 기댔다.

"......"

"You don't feel like that?"

They looked at each other. Yeong-sun said, "Teacher, we don't feel that way. There are so many things to do..."

"Anyway, I'd like to think hard. In order to begin again, you know."

"What would you begin again?" asked Cheol-sun.

Yun didn't answer, took out a cigarette and lit it. After he exhaled, a long trail of smoke hung in the air. He looked at the print.

He said, "That's an unusual picture."

"It's Jeon Tae-il, the martyr," answered Misuk.

"A new style. Is art changing, too?"

"I don't know about art. I heard that the artist who made this print participated in the May struggle as well. What he was trying to say was clear, and affordable as well."

When Misuk finished talking, Yeong-sun proudly said, "I also have the same print."

After looking around the room, Yun looked at the picture again. He said, "It's strangely moving to see that picture in this room. It feels as if the picture ran out of a gallery or living room and is shouting at the world."

"피곤하실 텐데 길게 누우세요." 하면서 윤강일의 옆쪽에 앉아 있던 영순이가 자리를 만들어주었다.

"괜찮아."

윤강일은 다시 몸을 곧추세웠다. 그는 생각에 잠기는 듯 표정이 골똘해졌다. 철순이가 빈 병과 담배꽁초를 비닐봉다리에 넣었다. 영순이는 창문을 열었다. 담배 연기가 빨려 나간다. 창문을 닫으며 영순이가 말했다.

"연탄불 좀 피워야겠구나."

"백 장 이상만 배달해주니…… 이달 봉급 때까지 그럭저럭 지내지 뭐."

"겨울 되면 살기가 더 빡빡해." 하는 말들이 오갔다. 윤강일이 말했다.

"그래도 잠수함 타는 사람들은 여름이 제일 죽겠다더라. 창문을 열 수도 없고. 그래도 올여름은 비가 많이 와서 그런대로 견딜 만했지."

"정말 비가 많이 왔어요."

미숙이의 말을 영순이가 받았다.

"이상한 소문도 많이 떠돌았고, 한동안 물 때문에 혼났어요. 물 색깔도 이상하고 콜레라가 휩쓸었잖아요. 알고 보니 수원지에 버린 시체가 썩었대요."

They were all looking at the picture. The burning body looked as if it was about to run right out of the picture. Finally, Misuk asked Yun, "Have you heard about Hyeong-ja?"

"I hope she's well?" asked Yun, turning his eyes away from the print. Nobody answered. Everyone stayed silent until he finished his cigarette. Watching him bringing a cup to his mouth, Sunbun said, in a low voice, "She died."

The cup froze in mid-air, then started shaking. It spilt a little *soju*. He put the cup down.

"She died? When? Where?"

"The last day at the governor's office building..."

Yun sat straight up. Then he muttered, "She... she..."

The smoke rising from his fingertips in a white line was shaking, too. He asked in a hoarse voice, "Did you find the body?"

"No," said Sunbun, looking at Misuk. Then, she said again, "Misuk's brother is missing, too."

Misuk's eyes immediately filled with up. Yun opened his mouth a little, but quickly closed it and bowed his head. A thin vein in his temple was trembling in his darkened face. He made a tight fist. Then, he opened his fist and picked up the cup. He

윤강일은 길게 누웠다. 졸음이 오는 눈을 비볐다. 잠기
는 듯한 목소리로 말했다.

"커다란 획이 확 그려지고 지나갔어."

"지나간 것이 아니라, 계속 이어지고 있지요."

순분이가 말했다. 그녀는 가방 속에 있는 공책을 꺼내
어 윤강일에게 보여줄까 하다가 그만두었다. 그는 눈을
감고 있었다. 미숙이가 하나뿐인 이불을 덮어주었다. 베
개를 받쳐주려고 조심스럽게 머리를 들었다. 그가 눈을
떴다.

"나 자는 게 아니야." 하면서 졸린 눈을 억지로 크게 떠
보였다. 창문 밖으로 발걸음 소리가 들리다가 이내 멀어
져 갔다.

"난 노동자라는 게 자랑스러워."

철순이가 말했다. 윤강일은 잠들어 있었다. 코를 가늘
게 골았다. 자는 얼굴이 평온하다. 그로부터 시선을 돌리
며 순분은 동료들을 바라보았다. 지금까지와 다른 그 무
엇이 얼굴들 위에 나타나 있었다.

"시작이야."

순분이가 말했다.

"없는 사람들이 끝까지 책임지고 투쟁을 했어. 그렇다

gulped three or four cups one after another. He lit his cigarette again. As if his body was receding like the smoke of the cigarette, he leaned against the wall listlessly.

"You must be tired. Please lie down," said Yeong-sun, making room for him next to her.

"It's ok."

Yun sat straight up again. As if deep in thought, he looked absorbed. Cheol-sun put the empty bottle and cigarette butts in the plastic bag. Yeong-sun opened the window. The cigarette smoke was being sucked out. Closing the window, Yeong-sun said, "we'd better light the briquettes."

"They deliver briquettes only when we order more than a hundred pieces... I'm hoping to get by until my payday this month."

"It gets harder to live during the winter."

Yun said, "Summer is really hard for those who go underground. You can't even open the window. Last summer was tolerable because it rained a lot."

"It really did rain a lot."

At Misuk's remark, Yeong-sun said, "There were strange rumors, too. It was very hard for a while also because of the water. Its color was strange, and cholera was rampant. It turned out that bodies

185

면 5월은 진짜 투쟁의 시작이야."

잠시 침묵이 흘렀다. 침묵 속에 그녀들은 서로 눈길을 주고받았다. 통과의 눈길이었다. 그 눈길 위에 한 목소리가 말하였다.

"그 연장 위에서 우리의 투쟁 목표는 분명해졌어."

윤강일이 한 발로 이불을 차냈다. 발에서 냄새가 났다. 미숙은 양말을 벗겨냈다. 점퍼도 벗겼다. 깃 부분이 새카맣다. 나가서 빨았다. 그녀들은 내일을 위해서 오지 않는 잠을 억지로 청했다.

새벽에 일어난 미숙이와 철순이는 구멍가게에 가서 배추 한 포기와 두부 세 모를 샀다. 배추 겉절이를 하고 두부찌개도 끓였다. 그녀들은 윤강일이 깰까 봐서 소리를 죽여가며 밥을 먹었다. 나갈 채비를 끝냈을 때 순분이가 말했다.

"선생님 돈도 없을 거야. 잠수함 타는 것이 얼마나 힘들겠니? 너희들 돈들 다 털어봐."

백 원짜리도 나왔고 오백 원짜리도 나왔다. 합해서 이천 원도 못 되었다. 순분은 주머니에서 돈을 꺼내 삼천 원을 만들었다. 미숙이가 공책을 찢어 글을 썼다.

thrown into the water source were polluting our drinking water."

Yun lay down. He rubbed his sleepy eyes. He said in a hoarse voice, "Somebody made one bold ink stroke, then disappeared."

"It didn't pass by. The stroke is continuing," said Sunbun.

She thought of showing him her notebook with all the numbers, but decided not to. He had already closed his eyes. Misuk covered him with the only blanket she had. In order to put a pillow under him, she carefully lifted his head. He opened his eyes.

"I'm not sleeping," he said, trying very hard to keep his drowsy eyes open. They could hear footsteps outside the window, but they soon receded.

"I'm proud to be a laborer," said Cheol-sun. Yun Gang-il was asleep. He was snoring slightly. His face looked peaceful. Sunbun turned her eyes toward her friends. Their faces looked different from before.

"Now is the beginning," said Sunbun.

"Have-nots took responsibility and fought until the end. May was the beginning of a real struggle."

There was silence for a while. They exchanged glances in silence. They were glances of a passage.

선생님, 피곤하신 것 같아 깨우지 못했습니다. 일어나시는 대로 진지 잡수세요. 찌개는 꼭 데워 잡수세요. 점퍼와 양말은 부엌에 널어 놓았어요. 남들이 볼까 봐서요. 덜마르면 다리미로 다려 입으세요. 다리미는 나무 궤짝 안에 있어요. 선생님, 오시고 싶을 때 언제라도 오세요. 부엌 선반 가운데에 엎어놓은 작은 종지가 있어요. 그곳에 열쇠가 있어요. 그럼 선생님, 편히 계세요.

돈을 넣은 봉투 속에 같이 넣었다. 그녀들은 밖으로 나왔다. 귀끝이 싸아하다. 골목을 걸어나가다가 순분이가 다시 뒤돌아서며 말했다.

"너희들 천천히 가고 있어. 잠깐 잊어먹은 게 있어서……"

대문을 밀었다. 부엌으로 갔다. 방문을 열었다. 발은 부엌에 둔 채로 팔을 뻗쳤다. 아까 그 봉투를 끄집어냈다. 안주머니에서 꼬깃꼬깃한 돈 삼천 원을 꺼냈다. 다 넣을까 하다가 천 원을 다시 호주머니에 넣고 이천 원만 봉투에 넣었다. 다시 밀어 넣었다. 윤강일이 몸을 뒤척였다. 깨어나는가 하고 잠시 머뭇거렸다. 어두컴컴한 방 그늘 속에 그는 계속 잠을 잤다. 순분은 소리 안 나게 방문을

A voice said over the glances, "The goal of our struggle became clearer. It is the extension of the May struggle."

Yun Gang-il kicked the blanket with his foot. It was smelly. Misuk took off his socks. She took off his jacket as well. Its collar was dirty. She took them out and washed them. They tried to sleep, although they were wide-awake.

Misuk and Cheol-sun woke up early in the morning and went to the corner store to buy a head of cabbage and three pieces of tofu. They pickled the cabbage and cooked a tofu *miso* soup. In order not to wake Yun Gang-il, they ate breakfast very quietly. When they were ready to leave, Sunbun said, "He probably doesn't have much money. How hard it must be to go underground! Give me all the money you have!"

They took out hundred dollar bills and five hundred dollar bills. All together, it was less than two thousand *won*. Sunbun took out more money from her pocket to make it three thousand *won*. Misuk tore a page from her notebook and wrote.

Teacher, we are not waking you up because you look tired. When you wake up, please have break-

조용히 닫았다.

　안개가 자욱이 끼어 있었다. 거리의 상가는 문 열 기미
도 없다. 그녀들은 천변을 따라 걸어갔다. 출근하는 근로
자들이 곳곳에 보였다. 천변을 지나자 큰 도로가 나왔다.
더 많은 근로자들이 보였다. 도로를 걷다 보면 왼쪽으로
꺾어지는 길이 나 있다. 길 끝 쪽에 공장의 철문이 활짝
열려 있다. 많은 근로자들이 행렬을 이루고 있다. 자전거
를 타고 출근하는 근로자도 있다. 그녀들 곁을 지나가는
남자 근로자들이 휘파람을 불었다. 그녀들은 미소 지었
다. 뒤에서 찌르룽 소리가 한꺼번에 울렸다. 근로자 서너
명이 자전거를 타고 달려오고 있었다. 길을 비켰다. 자전
거들이 다가왔다. 그녀들 곁을 지나면서 한 근로자가 말
했다.
　"뒤에 타세요."
　그녀들은 웃으면서 고개를 저었다. 뒤쪽에 도시락 가방
이 꽁꽁 묶여 있었다. 그가 힘껏 페달을 밟았다. 새벽 공
기를 가르며 달려갔다. 증기기관차의 김처럼 입김을 씩씩
뿜어내며 힘차게 달려갔다.
　머리카락이 휘날렸다. 작업복 자락이 펄럭였다. 점점

fast. Please heat the soup before you eat. Your jacket and socks are drying in the kitchen. We didn't want others to see. If they didn't dry completely, please iron and wear them. The iron is in the wooden box. Teacher, please visit whenever you can. There is a tiny bowl in the middle of a shelf in the kitchen. You'll find a key under it. Teacher, take good care of yourself.

She put it in an envelope with the money. They went out. The tops of their ears were chilly. Walking down the alley, Sunbun suddenly turned around and said, "Keep going slowly. I forgot something..."

She pushed the door in and entered the kitchen. She opened the door of the room. Standing in the kitchen, she stretched out her arm. She took the envelope and took out three thousand *won* from the inside pocket of her coat. She thought of putting all of it into the envelope, but changed her mind. She put a thousand *won* back in her pocket and added the remaining two thousand *won* to the envelope. Then, she pushed the envelope into the room. Yun Gang-il tossed about. Wondering if he was waking up, she lingered briefly. In the dark

멀어지면서 새벽 여명 속에 옷자락의 펄럭임만이 보였다.

수없는 펄럭임이었다. 그것은 깃발이었다.

1) 캐터필러(caterpillar) : 차바퀴의 둘레에 강판으로 만든 벨트를
   걸어 놓은 장치. 무한궤도.
2) 타이밍(timing) : 각성제의 상표명.
3) 카키(khaki)색 : 누른빛을 띤 엷은 갈색. 주로 군복에 많이 씀.
4) 선라이트(sunlight) : 반투명해서 빛이 들어오도록 만든 플라스틱
   건축 자재. 예전에 지붕용으로 많이 쓰였음.
5) 언더(under) : '언더그라운드(underground)'의 줄임말. 비합법
   적인 지하운동. 또는 그 지하운동을 하는 단체.
6) 행불(行不) : 행방불명.

『깃발』, 창비, 2003(1988)

corner of the room, he continued to sleep. Sunbun quietly closed the door.

The fog was thick. None of the stores on the street were open. They walked along the riverbank. Laborers were going to their workplaces here and there. After the riverbank, they arrived at a broad street. There were more laborers. After a while the road turned left. At the end was an iron gate that was wide open. Workers were entering in a procession. Some were riding bicycles. Male workers were whistling, as they passed by. They smiled. Many bells were ringing behind them at the same time. Some workers on bicycles must be in a hurry. They stepped aside. The bicycles approached. Passing by them, a worker offered, "Please jump on back!"

Smiling, they shook their heads. A lunch box was tightly tied on the back of the bicycle. The man sped up. His bicycle zoomed forward, slicing the early morning air in half. His breath spurting out like vapor from a steam locomotive, he pedaled forcefully.

His hair was fluttering. The hem of his uniform was fluttering. As he got further and further away, only the fluttering hem of his clothes was visible in

the gray of the morning. Innumerable flutterings...
like a flag.

1) Sunlight is a brand name of a semitransparent plastic panel.
2) *Pyeong* is a Korean measure of area, equal to 3.954 square yards and *majigi* is a Korean measure of farmland, equal to 0.12-0.16 acres.
3) BG means bourgeoisie and PT proletariat.
4) "Eonni" means older sister. In Korean, women often call an older female friend "Eonni."
5) "Hyeong" means brother. A title for one's own older brother, it is often used for older male friends as well.
6) Jeon Tae-il is an iconic South Korean labor activist who burned himself to death to protest against unjust labor practices in Cheonggye area garment factories in 1970; Seok Jeong-nam is a female labor activist of the 1970's and the author of a memoir entitled *Light in the Factory*.
7) "Burning Tears" is the title of an essay Seok Jeong-nam published in the magazine, *Dialogue*.
8) The JOC is the Korean branch of the international Catholic labor network.
9) The Songbaek Association is an organization that helped political prisoners.
10) Koreans sometimes call Caucasians "big-nose people" pejoratively.
11) "Nuna" is a name used by a man for an elder sister. Men sometimes use it for an older female friend.
12) Timing and Bacchus are brand names of antihypnotic drugs.
13) This phrase is a quote from a well-known poem written by Yun Dong-ju during the Japanese colonial period.
14) "A Moon village" is a name for a crowded residential area

where poor people live in houses built illegally. It is called a "Moon" village because most of these areas are on a hill, which is closer to the Moon.

Translated by Jeon Seung-hee

해설

Afterword

뜨거웠던 그 해 5월을 증언하다

이정현(문학평론가)

1979년 10월 26일, 박정희 대통령이 암살당했다. 18년 간의 군부 독재에서 벗어난 한국은 민주화에 대한 기대가 커져갔다. 이듬해인 1980년 봄, 전국 각지에서 민주화 요구 시위가 거세졌다. 그러나 정권을 장악하기 시작한 신군부는 민주화 요구를 묵살했고, 1980년 5월 광주에서 벌어진 민주화 시위는 전두환 장군이 파견한 공수부대에 의해 진압되었다. 공수부대에 맞서서 저항하던 시민들은 잔혹하게 학살당했고, 전두환의 신군부는 정권 수립을 위한 발판을 마련했다. 홍희담의 소설 「깃발」은 1980년 5월의 광주를 무대로 삼고 있다. 그 해 5월의 열흘 동안 노동자와 학생을 포함한 광주의 시민들은 스스로 '시민군'이란

Testimony for the Burning May of 1980

Lee Jeong-hyeon (literary critic)

President Park Chung-hee was assassinated on October 26, 1979. Just released from an eighteen-year military dictatorship, the Korean people were increasingly hopeful that their society would be democratized. In the spring of 1980, demonstrators across the country were demanding democratization. But the military junta that had just seized power ignored the people's yearning for democracy. In May 1980, General Chun Doo-hwan sent airborne troops to suppress demonstrations in Gwangju. Citizens who resisted the troops were ruthlessly massacred, and the new military junta led by General Chun cleared the way for the establish-

명칭을 사용하면서 자신들의 세금으로 운용되는 군대와 대치했다.

작품 속에는 순분, 형자, 두칠 등 노동자들과 지식인 윤강일이 등장한다. 작가는 노동자와 지식인 계급을 대표하는 등장인물들을 통해서 광주 안에서 벌어진 또 하나의 대립을 보여준다. 도청에서 마지막 전투를 앞두고 두 계층은 다른 태도를 취한다. 운동권 지도부에 속해 있던 지식인 윤강일은 제일 먼저 도피한다. 윤강일이 내뱉는 말들은 이렇다. 혁명, 비지(부르주아), 피티(프롤레타리아), 전사(戰士), 빨치산, 무장투쟁, 계급투쟁, 시가전, 유격전, 죽창, 게릴라, 봉기, 제국주의, 자본주의, 주변부 자본주의, 종속이론, 해방신학, 제3세계, 민중, 프랑스혁명, 파리코뮌, 러시아혁명, 레닌, 볼셰비키, 베트남, 통일 등 '매력적인' 언어다. 그는 항쟁 초기, 시위대를 선동해 MBC(문화방송) 건물을 불태운다. 그러나 진압군이 발포를 시작하자마자, "어차피 지는 싸움"이라며 광주를 떠난다. 윤강일의 제자이면서 노동자인 형자는 분노에 차 항의한다. "어떻게 그럴 수가 있어요? 선생님들이 말하던 시가전, 봉기 등등이 나오고 있는데……." 결국 마지막까지 도청에 남은 자들은 대부분 하층민들이었다. 어떤 이득이나 명예를

ment of his new regime. "The Flag" by Hong Hee-dam is a story set in Gwangju during that month of May. For ten days, citizens of Gwangju, including laborers and students, calling themselves a "citizen army," and fought against the military sustained by their own taxes.

The main characters of this story include labor-ers—Sunbun, Hyeong-ja, and Du-chil—and intellec-tuals—Yun Gang-il and others. Hong presents another kind of confrontation within Gwangju by contrasting these two classes of people who took different positions in the last battle at the governor's office complex. Yun Gang-il, an intellectual and leader of the Gwangju democracy movement, is the first to run away. He used to enjoy using such words as "Revolution," "BG," "PT," "fighter," "parti-san," "armed struggle," "class struggle," "street fight-ing," "guerrilla fighting," "bamboo spears," "guerril-las," "revolt," "imperialism," "capitalism," "marginal capitalism," "theory of dependence," "liberation the-ology," "the third world," "people," "French Revolution," "Paris Commune," "Russian Revolution," "Lenin," "Bolshevik," "Vietnam," "unifi-cation," etc. They were all very "attractive" terms. In the beginning of the resistance, he led demonstra-

바라지 않으면서도 서로를 돕고 목숨까지 바치는 노동자들의 순수한 모습은 지식인들의 비겁함과 대비된다. 작가는 작품 속에서 노동자의 입을 빌려 자신의 주장을 직설적으로 드러낸다.

"도청에 끝까지 남아 있던 사람들을 잘 기억해둬. 어떤 사람이 항쟁에 가담했고 투쟁했고 죽었는가를 꼭 기억해야 돼. 그러면 너희들은 알게 될 거야. 어떤 사람들이 역사를 쓰는지."

"시작이야. 없는 사람들이 끝까지 책임지고 투쟁을 했어. 그렇다면 5월은 진짜 투쟁의 시작이야. 그 연장 위에서 우리의 투쟁 목표는 분명해졌어."

항쟁이 끝난 후에도 노동자들은 도피했던 지식인 윤강일을 오히려 도와준다. 그리고 삶에 대한 의지를 포기하지 않고 일터로 향한다. 일터로 향하는 노동자들의 작업복이 바람에 펄럭이는 모습을 작가는 이렇게 적는다. "그것은 깃발이었다." 이렇듯 작가는 뚜렷하게 대비되는 두 계층의 태도를 통해서 노동자들의 순수함과 질긴 생명력

tors to the MBC building to burn it down. However, the moment the military begins shooting protestors, he sneaks away from Gwangju, saying, "This is a losing battle." Hyeong-ja, his student and a laborer, protests in anger, "How could you? ... This is the very situation of a street fight, revolt, etc., that you teachers have always been talking about..." In the end it is mostly lower class people who end up staying in the governor's office complex. The author presents the pure heart of laborers who help each other and dedicate their lives to the greater cause without expecting any profit or honor in return in clear contrast with the cowardice exhibited by intellectuals. A character in the story argues:

"Do remember those who stayed in the governor's office building complex to the last? You must remember those who took part in this struggle and died... Then, you'll know who makes history."

"Now is the beginning... Have-nots took responsibility and fought until the end. May was the beginning of a real struggle. The goal of our struggle became clearer. It is the extension of the May struggle."

이야말로 사회를 변혁시키는 힘이라고 주장한다. 동시에 고립된 광주에서 벌어진 학살을 생생하게 고발한다. 작가는 지속적으로 광주를 화두로 삼으면서 다양한 계층의 시선과 함께 살아남은 자의 고통을 담은 작품도 지속적으로 발표했다.

한국의 1980년대는 엄혹한 시기였다. 수많은 사람들이 구속되고 감시당했으며, 『깃발』이 발표된 1988년까지도 고립된 광주에서 벌어진 학살은 그 진상조차 명확히 밝혀지지 않았다. 따라서 광주의 참상을 고발하기 위해 많은 작가들이 활발하게 움직였다. 홍희담의 「깃발」은 그 시발점이 된 작품이다. 이후 임철우의 『봄날』, 송기숙의 『오월의 미소』, 문순태의 『그들의 새벽』, 정찬의 『광야』, 『슬픔의 강』, 황지우의 『오월의 신부』 등 광주를 다룬 많은 작품들이 등장했다.

한편 이 작품을 통해서 우리는 1980년대 문학의 특징과 한계를 알 수 있다. 홍희담이 지속적으로 응시했던 '광주'는 1980년대 문학을 형성시키고 그 성격을 규정하게 만든 원체험이었다. 1980년 광주항쟁 이후 문학은 독재의 탄압에 맞선 투쟁에서 특정한 역할을 담당해야 된다고 여기는 경향이 강했다. 홍희담의 「깃발」 역시 정교한 문학작품이

After the resistance, laborers even help Yun Gang-il on the run. Without giving up their will to live, they go to work. Hong describes the flutterings of the work clothes the laborers wear as "innumerable flutterings... like a flag." By presenting this contrast in attitudes between the two classes, the author argues that the pure heart, persistence, and vitality of laborers are a driving force for social change. At the same time, this short story is a vivid indictment of the massacres that happened in isolated Gwangju in May 1980. Since her publication of "The Flag," Hong has continued to publish stories about Gwangju, embodying not only the perspectives of various classes but also the pain of survivors.

The 1980s in Korea were a dark age. Many people were arrested and under police surveillance. The truth of the massacres in isolated Gwangju was not clearly known until 1988, when "The Flag" was first published. Hong's "The Flag" was the starting point of efforts by many writers to tell the truth. Lim Chul-woo's *Spring Days*, Song Gi-suk's *May Smile*, Mun Sun-tae's *Their Dawn*, Jeong-Chan's *Wilderness and River of Sadness*, and Hwang Ji-u's *May Bride* all followed in the footsteps of "The Flag."

"The Flag" is characteristic of Korean literature in

라기보다는 변혁운동의 필요성을 강조하는 '프로파간다'
나 '항쟁 보고서'의 성격이 짙다. 이것은 은폐된 진실을
밝히기 위한 '폭로'와 사회변혁을 위한 '계몽'과 '실천'이
1980년대의 화두였기 때문이다. 그러므로 1980년대 문학
은 사건의 전개가 지나치게 도식적이며 계급편향적인 작
품들이 많다. 이렇듯 1980년대의 문학은 민주화 투쟁에
큰 기여를 했지만, 작품성의 한계 또한 명확하다. 홍희담
의 「깃발」은 그러한 1980년대 문학의 상징적인 작품이다.

the 1980s in its nature and limitations. "Gwangju," on which Hong persistently focused, was the archetypal experience of the 1980s that characterized and defined the literature of this period. After the Gwangju Uprising in 1980, many thought that literature should play a significant role in the people's resistance to dictatorial oppression. Hong's "The Flag" is more like a work of "propaganda" for a revolutionary movement or a "report on the uprising" than a high art: this is evident in the use of such key words of 1980s' literature as "disclosure" of covered-up truth and "enlightenment" and "activism" for social change. Korean literature in the 1980s tended to emphasize "class" and have schematic narratives. It contributed greatly to the people's struggle for democracy, although it may not be artistically refined. Hong's "The Flag" is symbolic of this kind of literature.

비평의 목소리

Critical Acclaim

학생을 중심으로 한 지식인 주도의 초기 국면에서 민중
주도로 넘어가는 항쟁의 실제적 변화과정을 노동자의 눈
으로 침통하게 묘파하며 광주민주화운동의 역사적 의미
를 재해석해냈다.

임규찬

　성장한 민중세력의 '각성된 눈'을 통해 객관적인 거리
를 갖고 쓰인 광주 소재 소설의 진전된 면모는 1988년 발
표된 홍희담의 「깃발」에서 비로소 발견할 수 있다. 계급
적인 시각에서 광주항쟁을 해석해 보인 이 소설은 건강한
민중과 낙관적 미래를 보여주는 노동소설의 전형으로 평

A serious and insightful description of the process of change that occurred within the uprising, its transition from the student-and-intellectual-led early phase to the people-led later phase, and a serious reinterpretation of the historical significance of the Gwangju democratization movement.

Im Gyu-chan

Hong Hee-dam's "The Flag" is the first story about Gwangju objectively presented and written from the perspective of the "awakened eyes" of people whose power was growing. An interpretation of the Gwangju Uprising in terms of class, this story is a

가된다. 여성 노동자의 일상적 삶에 대한 생생한 기록, 노동자 중심의 민주화운동에 대한 강렬한 지향성, 1980년대 후반에 타올랐던 노동운동의 조직적 전개에 대한 낙관적 진단을 담아낸 이 소설은 노동문학이 이루어낸 뛰어난 성과라 할 수 있다.

백지연

만약 '5월 문학'이란 말에 가장 적합한 작가를 들라면 당연히 홍희담을 들 수밖에 없을 정도로 5월을 소설 쓰기의 유일한 화두로 여겨온 작가이다. 「깃발」은 그중에서도 비교적 이른 시기에 80년 5월의 광주항쟁을 '총체적인' 시각에서 써낸 문제작이다. (……) 이 작품에서 홍희담은 반미·통일·민주주의라는 80년대의 세 가지 주요 화두가 광주항쟁에서부터 광범위하게 대중화되기 시작했음을 의식적으로 부각시키고 있다.

김형중

「깃발」은 광주항쟁의 현장에 참여한 노동자를 주인공으로 하여 광주항쟁의 성격과 의미를 재조명하고, 실패를 극복하기 위한 전망을 제시하고 있다. 이 작품은 노동자

prototype of working-class literature depicting people's healthy attitudes towards life and optimism about the future. "The Flag" is a great achievement of working-class literature with its vivid description of the daily lives of women workers, its serious orientation toward a working-class-led democratization movement, and its optimistic prognosis for the development of an organized labor movement, which materialized in the late 1980s.

Baek Ji-yeon

"May" has been the only keyword for the author, Hong Hee-dam. If we seek an author whose work is best described as "May literature," she has no rival. An early example of this literature, "The Flag" is a major achievement that "comprehensively" represents the Gwangju Uprising in May 1980 ... In this story, Hong underscores the fact that the three keywords of the 1980s—"anti-American," "unification," and "democracy"—began spreading among ordinary people in the Gwangju Uprising.

Kim Hyeong-jung

"The Flag" illuminates the nature and significance of the Gwangju Uprising and suggests ways to over-

의 시각에 고정되어 있음에도 불구하고 구체적 생활의 부재, 사건 전개의 도식성 등의 결함을 안고 있다. 그러나 다른 소설들에서 보여지는 피해자로서의 자기 인식에서 벗어나 역사 속에서의 자기 발견을 위한 노력을 보여준다는 점에서 뚜렷한 성격을 드러낸다. 이것은 권력 이데올로기의 비도덕성에 초점을 두고 있기에 그 피해자로서의 비극성이 강조되고 있는 여타의 소설에서 한걸음 나아가게 하는 요소이다. 비극성의 강조는 광주항쟁의 근본적인 발발원인에 대한 이성적인 접근을 방해하는 것 중의 하나란 점에서다.

신덕룡

come its limitations by highlighting the workers who participated in it. Although the story faithfully follows events seen through the eyes of workers, it doesn't offer full descriptions of their daily lives. The story also appears to follow a predetermined scheme. Despite these shortcomings, "The Flag" stands out in its depiction of workers as people who own their lives in history rather than simply accept their fate as victims. This is progress from other stories that only emphasize the victimhood of laborers and its tragic nature in order to criticize the immorality of the dominant ideology. If we only emphasize the tragic nature of the Gwangju Uprising, we will not be able to approach its root causes rationally.

Shin Deok-ryong

홍희담

홍희담은 1945년 9월 12일 서울에서 출생했다. 이화여대 국어국문학과를 졸업했다. 대학 졸업 후 남편을 따라 전라남도로 내려갔으며 1978년 광주로 이사했다. 한 남자의 아내와 두 아이의 어머니로 평범한 나날을 보내던 작가는 1980년 5월의 광주항쟁을 목격하게 된다. 광주의 학살을 목격한 이후 작가의 삶은 바뀌기 시작했다. 지옥과 같은 학살과 시민들이 나눴던 뜨거운 인간애를 동시에 마주한 작가는 광주의 체험을 결코 잊지 않겠다고 다짐한다. 1988년 《창작과 비평》에 광주항쟁을 정면으로 조명한 작품 「깃발」을 발표한 이후 작가로 활동하기 시작했으며 이후 발표된 작품들도 모두 '1980년 5월'을 반영했다.

많은 이들에게 광주는 지나간 과거지만 홍희담에게는 여전히 광주의 비극은 현재적이다. 2003년 발간된 소설집 『깃발』에는 표제작 「깃발」을 비롯하여 「그대에게 보내는 편지」 「문 밖에서」 「김치를 담그며」 「이제금 저 달이」가 실려 있다. 광주의 생생한 현장을 기록하고 있는 「깃발」을 제외한 나머지 작품들은 광주에서 살아남은 자들의 이

Hong Hee-dam

Hong Hee-dam was born in Seoul on September 12, 1945. After graduating from the Department of Korean Language and Literature at Ewha Womans University, she first moved to Jeollanam-do and then to Gwangju in 1978 with her husband. While living an ordinary housewife's life as the mother of two children in Gwangju, she witnessed the Gwangju Uprising in May 1980. After this event, she promised herself that she would never forget the hellish massacres and passionately humane love shared among citizens. After publishing "The Flag," a short story directly illuminating the Gwangju Uprising, in *Quarterly Changbi* in 1988, she has continued to publish stories about "May 1980."

Although Gwangju is in the past for many people, the tragedy of Gwangju is still present to Hong Hee-dam. Her collection of short stories entitled *The Flag* includes not only "The Flag," but also "Letter to Thee," "Outside the Door," "Making Kimchi," and "That Moon, Until Now." Except for "The Flag," a vivid description of the Gwangju uprising itself, the

야기다. 광주의 비극을 원죄처럼 안고 살아가는 자들의 고통을 통해서 작가는 화해와 치유의 가능성을 모색한다. 특히 1990년대 이후의 작품 속에서는 비극을 겪은 이후에도 여전히 자식을 낳고, 삶의 희망을 포기하지 않는 여성들이 등장한다. 그 여성들을 통해서 작가는 과거의 비극이 남긴 상처가 어떻게 치유될 수 있는지를 묻는다.

광주의 비극을 다루던 작가는 2011년 『별에도 가고 투발루에도 가고』라는 장편동화를 출간한다. 이제 손자들에게 사랑받는 할머니가 된 작가는 광주의 비극을 넘어서 미래의 희망을 말한다. 할머니로서 손녀들을 보살피면서 겪고 살핀 작가의 시선은 따뜻한 연민의 모성으로 가득 차 있다. 많은 작품을 발표하지는 않았지만 홍희담의 작품세계의 변화는 상처의 치유 과정과 닮았다. 역사와 개인의 비극을 지속적으로 다루던 작가는 이제 연민과 모성이 담긴 눈으로 새로운 세대를 바라보고 있다.

other stories focus on Gwangju survivors. The author explores the possibility of reconciliation and healing in her stories of survivors living with painful feelings of guilt for the tragedy in Gwangju. In particular, her stories published after the 1990s feature women who raise children without giving up hope in life. She addresses the question of how we can heal the wounds of a past tragedy.

Hong, a beloved grandmother now, published a long children's book in 2011, *To Stars, to Tubalu*, a book about hope for the future. This story is filled with a warm and sympathetic maternity that comes from the author's own experience of taking care of her grandchildren. Although she is not prolific, Hong's process of development as a writer resembles the healing of a wound. Having persisted in writing about historical and personal tragedies, she is now turning her compassionate and maternal glance toward new generations.

번역 전승희 Translated by Jeon Seung-hee

서울대학교와 하버드대학교에서 영문학과 비교문학으로 박사 학위를 받았으며, 현재 하버드대학교 한국학 연구소의 연구원으로 재직하며 아시아 문예 계간지 《ASIA》 편집위원으로 활동 중이다. 현대 한국문학 및 세계문학을 다룬 논문을 다수 발표했으며, 바흐친의 『장편소설과 민중언어』, 제인 오스틴의 『오만과 편견』 등을 공역했다. 1988년 한국여성연구소의 창립과 《여성과 사회》의 창간에 참여했고, 2002년부터 보스턴 지역 피학대 여성을 위한 단체인 '트랜지션하우스' 운영에 참여해 왔다. 2006년 하버드대학교 한국학 연구소에서 '한국 현대사와 기억'을 주제로 한 워크숍을 주관했다.

Jeon Seung-hee is a member of the Editorial Board of ASIA, is a Fellow at the Korea Institute, Harvard University. She received a Ph.D. in English Literature from Seoul National University and a Ph.D. in Comparative Literature from Harvard University. She has presented and published numerous papers on modern Korean and world literature. She is also a co-translator of Mikhail Bakhtin's *Novel and the People's Culture* and Jane Austen's *Pride and Prejudice*. She is a founding member of the Korean Women's Studies Institute and of the biannual Women's Studies' journal *Women and Society* (1988), and she has been working at 'Transition House', the first and oldest shelter for battered women in New England. She organized a workshop entitled "The Politics of Memory in Modern Korea" at the Korea Institute, Harvard University, in 2006. She also served as an advising committee member for the Asia-Africa Literature Festival in 2007 and for the POSCO Asian Literature Forum in 2008.

감수 K. E. 더핀 Edited by K. E. Duffin

시인, 화가, 판화가. 하버드 인문대학원 글쓰기 지도 강사를 역임하고, 현재 프리랜서 에디터, 글쓰기 컨설턴트로 활동하고 있다.

K. E. Duffin is a poet, painter and printmaker. She is currently working as a freelance editor and writing consultant as well. She was a writing tutor for the Graduate School of Arts and Sciences, Harvard University.

바이링궐 에디션 한국 현대 소설 019

깃발

2013년 6월 10일 초판 1쇄 인쇄 | 2013년 6월 15일 초판 1쇄 발행

지은이 홍희담 | **옮긴이** 전승희 | **펴낸이** 방재석
감수 K. E. 더핀 | **기획** 정은경, 전성태, 이경재
편집 정수인, 이은혜, 이윤정 | **관리** 박신영 | **디자인** 이춘희

펴낸곳 아시아 | **출판등록** 2006년 1월 31일 제319-2006-4호
주소 서울특별시 동작구 흑석동 100-16
전화 02.821.5055 | **팩스** 02.821.5057 | **홈페이지** www.bookasia.org
ISBN 978-89-94006-73-4 (set) | 978-89-94006-77-2 (04810)
값은 뒤표지에 있습니다.
이 책은 저작권자와 (주)창비의 동의하에 발행합니다.

Bi-lingual Edition Modern Korean Literature 019
The Flag

Written by Hong Hee-dam | **Translated by** Jeon Seung-hee
Published by Asia Publishers | 100-16 Heukseok-dong, Dongjak-gu, Seoul, Korea
Homepage Address www.bookasia.org | **Tel.** (822).821.5055 | **Fax.** (822).821.5057
First published in Korea by Asia Publishers 2013
ISBN 978-89-94006-73-4 (set) | 978-89-94006-77-2 (04810)